The Hot Spurs

When the riders of the Bar 10 run up against an escaped prisoner and his ruthless gang they find themselves in deep trouble. Bret Jarvis and his henchmen are heading to Mexico when they learn that the Circle J ranch have returned from a profitable cattle drive and are heavy with loot, making them a sitting target for a raid.

But Gene Adams and his Bar 10 cowboys are soon in hot pursuit and all they need to do is stop the outlaws before they reach the border. . . .

The Hot Spurs

Boyd Cassidy

A Black Horse Western

ROBERT HALE · LONDON

© Boyd Cassidy 2013
First published in Great Britain 2013

ISBN 978-0-7198-0992-7

Robert Hale Limited
Clerkenwell House
Clerkenwell Green
London EC1R 0HT

www.halebooks.com

Typeset by
Derek Doyle & Associates, Shaw Heath
Printed and bound in Great Britain by
CPI Antony Rowe, Chippenham and Eastbourne

ONE

There was a low sun which was getting lower with every beat of the eleven riders' black hearts as they sat amid the rocks to either side of the solitary route in and out of the ancient adobe prison. Los Angelo had stood since the first Spanish missionaries had built it as a place of worship. A place where they thought they might be able to tame the natives. It had not worked and some said its high walls were stained with the blood which had been spilled there. The array of buildings had survived the ravages of the Texas wilderness for more than a century until it had been turned into a temporary prison. That had been the Texas Rangers' first mistake. The second had been to send the notorious gang leader Cole Logan there and think its walls could hold him.

Darkness came swiftly as the sun finally disappeared behind the mountains. Logan's gang were well trained and knew when and where to strike. Knew when their target was at its weakest and most vulnerable.

Their leader had taught them well. Each and every one of them was as merciless as Logan himself. They took no prisoners and left no witnesses.

The bodies of the four prison guards who had set out for provisions earlier that day still lay where they had fallen amid their horses and pack-mules deep in the maze of gigantic boulders. Death had come quickly and silently.

Those who remained in the prison were oblivious to what had occurred less than a quarter mile from the prison's high adobe walls and solid gates. Now reduced to a mere five men including the warden they had no idea of what was about to occur as the moonless night grew ever darker.

Two guards patrolled the walls to either side of the gates and looked down at the courtyard where torches lit up the sand and the cells that faced the expanse of sand. Into a dozen putrid cells, which were exposed to the elements, were crammed two hundred of the most dangerous criminals in the state. The guards' carbines were always aimed at the cells and the prisoners who clung to their bars.

That was their third mistake.

For if they had turned their rifles to face the blackness beyond the prison's walls they might have had a chance of picking off some of the eleven horsemen as they silently approached the remote Los Angelo. Yet as with all men who are charged with guarding prisoners they consider training their weaponry on unarmed creatures. They never consider that the real danger lies not with those who are already locked up but with those who have yet to be caught and brought to justice. The true danger is the deadly well-armed outlaws who are still free. Free to shoot back.

Rem Barker had long been Cole Logan's top gun. He alone amongst the eleven members of the infamous gang knew exactly what his leader wanted and why he wanted it. Even before the Rangers had transported Logan to the remote prison set on the eastern fringes of the Lone Star state Barker had known that if he and the other members of the deadly gang ever expected to rob another bank successfully they would have to free their leader.

Cole Logan might have been one of the most merciless men ever to have lived but he had made each and every one of them wealthy. He had a genius when it came to robbing banks. Without him Barker knew they were all doomed. An army without its general was nothing.

The riders held their horses on short rein as they allowed them to canter towards the high adobe walls. Each had his own job to do. Each would do it expertly.

The soft sand muffled the sound of their hoofs as their mounts gathered pace and closed in on their objective. Barker turned to the closest riders on either side of him and gave a silent signal. Both riders pulled their cutting-ropes free and started to swing them above their heads. Barker himself reached the gates first and drew rein. He then reached back to his saddle-bags and pulled a half-dozen sticks of dynamite free. They were tied together with a short two-minute fuse protruding from the centre of the lethal bundle.

Apart from Barker and the two rope men the rest of the riders rode to the end of the front wall as Barker scratched a match with his thumbnail and lit the fuse. He then dropped the explosives at the foot of the large gates and turned his mount. Barker rode past the two outlaws with the swinging ropes in their hands.

'Now!' he ordered.

The horsemen swung their ropes, then released the wide loops up into the air. Each lasso went around the neck of a guard far above them, then jerked tight. Faster than the blink of an eye the outlaws wrapped the ends of their ropes around their saddle horns and spurred. Before either of the prison guards could utter a word they were suddenly hauled over the edge of the wall. They fell backwards and came crashing down to the sand. The sound of their necks breaking rang out. Their limp bodies were then dragged to where Barker and the eight other gang members waited.

When the pair of riders reached Barker and their cohorts they released their ropes. The guard's broken bodies lay mangled.

'Wait for it.' Rem Barker said, watching the solitary entrance of the prison.

The massive explosion turned the solid gates into a million splinters. The dust had barely cleared when the eleven horsemen galloped into the prison courtyard with guns drawn.

The warden and the remaining prison guards stood no chance as they emerged from their quarters.

Blazing six-shooters spewed their fury across the torchlit courtyard. The warden raised his rifle and was brutally punched off his feet by a salvo of outlaw lead that came from half of the horsemen. No sooner had the large man hit the sand when those who remained of his guards found themselves cut to ribbons by even more rifle power. Each of them crashed into the ground like a ragdoll. Not one shot had been returned by any of the men charged with guarding the remote prison.

Barker raised his gun and signalled to his followers that their brief battle was over. The horsemen hauled rein and sat astride their mounts, watching Barker as he holstered his smoking .45.

'Find Cole,' Barker ordered as scores of desperate prisoners screamed out from their cells at the deadly intruders. Smouldering cinders floated down over the heavily armed horsemen. It was raining fire.

'Rem.' Cole Logan's voice bellowed out from one of the overcrowded cells. 'I'm over here, Rem. Get me out of here.'

Barker swung his mount around. His eyes narrowed and peered through the choking dust. Then he saw their leader clinging to the bars of a cell flanked by a score of other prisoners. He rode up to the cell and aimed his .45 at the lock. He squeezed its trigger. A deafening blast spewed from the barrel of the Colt. The large iron lock shattered into fragments. Along with Logan the other caged prisoners pushed the barred door open and ran out into the courtyard.

Logan ran out to his men. The other prisoners followed.

Barker lowered his left hand, caught hold of his leader's arm and dragged Logan off the ground. He swung Logan up behind him. The older outlaw sat behind the saddle cantle and hung on as Barker steadied his mount.

'What'll we do with these other prisoners, Cole?' Barker asked the man behind him.

With cold merciless eyes Cole Logan stared at the men with whom he had shared a cell. They were frantically trying to climb up behind the other mounted outlaws. That was not part of Logan's plan.

11

'Kill them,' Logan snarled into Barker's ear. 'Kill the whole stinking bunch of them.'

TWO

The rolling hillside was covered in a blanket of bluebonnet flowers which stretched for as far as the eye could see. The tall figure of the silver-haired rancher stood silently amid them, holding his black ten-gallon hat in his rugged gloved hands as though in silent prayer. He had not moved for more than an hour apart from the occasional turn of his head as he studied the tranquil scenery that surrounded him. This was a sacred place to Gene Lon Adams. A place where the dead rested beneath a canopy of a million blue flowers. The place where his beloved sweetheart had been laid to rest so very long before. Over the years that had followed that tragic event he had buried many of his loyal cowboys beneath the bluebonnets if they had no kinfolk to claim their broken bodies.

Far below the hillside his chestnut mare patiently waited as she had done countless times before. She would not move or stray until the rancher finished his silent ritual and returned to her. It was as if the handsome horse could actually read her master's mind. There was no hurry in either the man nor the beast. Some things required time.

Adams always came to this remote part of the Bar 10 ranch when he was troubled or when, as now, he was about to set out on a cattle drive. Unlike her master the horse heard the two horsemen approaching and turned her head to watch the familiar cowboys as they rode up to her.

Johnny Puma reined in and leapt from his saddle. He held on to the long leathers of his pinto pony and waited for the elderly Tomahawk to reach him. The older rider drew back and then carefully dismounted beside the youngster and gave a knowing nod.

'I told ya we'd find him here,' Tomahawk said.

'Reckon you did,' Johnny admitted. 'I figured as much myself. I just never said it.'

'Hold on a dang minute there, boy.' Tomahawk

screwed up his wrinkled features and moved to the smiling Johnny. His beard jutted at the young cowboy as though pointing. 'You wanted to go to town. You said Gene would be there, not here as I recall.'

Johnny grinned. 'I was thinking of you, old-timer. I was thinking, if we went to town you could go looking for Gene in one of the saloons. You could have had a beer or two.'

The bushy eyebrows of the seasoned old cowboy rose. 'Why didn't ya say that before, ya young whippersnapper? I *am* a leetle bit thirsty, now I thinks about it.'

Johnny touched the old man's arm and pointed at the rancher. Adams remained like a statue set in the middle of the knee-high bluebonnets.

'Gene sure is quiet, Tomahawk. How come?'

'He always is when he comes here.' Tomahawk sighed heavily and shook his head sadly. 'He's thinking on all the cowboys we buried here over the years. He's also thinking about his old sweetheart.'

Johnny looked down at the skinny figure. 'Gene had himself a sweetheart?'

'Yep.' Tomahawk nodded and then thoughtfully smiled at his younger companion. 'Prettiest thing

15

ya ever set eyes upon, Johnny. She was the love of his life.'

'What happened to her?'

'Injuns,' Tomahawk answered. 'They didn't cotton to folks invading their land. We was scouting for a wagon train and when we was off to the north looking for water for the oxen and horses the train was attacked. Killed them all.'

Johnny rubbed his neck. 'Killed them all? How many folks were in the wagon train?'

'Too many, boy.' Tomahawk looked at the ground. 'Way too many. We buried them all here. That's why Gene stayed here and we set up the ranch. She's buried somewhere around here. Gene knows where he buried her. She sure was pretty, Johnny.'

Johnny exhaled. 'What was her name?'

Tomahawk looked into the face of the younger man. 'Amy.'

The name had no sooner left the old-timer's lips than Gene turned and started to walk down the slope towards them. The morning sun rested on his broad unbending shoulders. As he approached he placed his wide-brimmed hat on his head of silver hair and tightened its drawstring. He did not look

16

at either of them as he navigated a course through the countless blue flowers. It was as if he did not want to step on any of them.

'Thought we'd find ya here, Gene boy.' Tomahawk said with a grin as the tall man reached them and his horse.

'Why you boys looking for me?' Adams asked, taking the reins of his mount. 'Something happened?'

Both men looked sheepish. Neither answered.

Adams held on to his saddle horn, poked a boot in a stirrup and then mounted his faithful horse. He sat looking at them.

'What happened?'

'Nothing happened, Gene,' Johnny bluffed.

Adams glanced at Tomahawk. 'Is Johnny telling the truth, old-timer?'

Both cowboys looked at one another, like two small children trying to work out whether they might be in serious trouble.

'We had us a leetle trouble with Cookie,' Tomahawk said at last. 'Just a leetle bit.'

Adams sucked in his cheeks. 'What kinda trouble?'

'He bust his leg,' Johnny quickly interrupted.

'What?' Adams voice rose. 'The man who is the most important part of the cattle drive has broken his leg? We can't start for McCoy with thousands of longhorns without a cook to wake and feed us. Cookie runs the whole show.'

Tomahawk waved his bony hands in the air. 'He only bust the one leg, Gene boy. Just the one.'

Johnny turned away.

Adams inhaled deeply. 'So we ain't got us a cook for the drive. Am I right?'

Tomahawk gave a slow nod. 'Yep.'

The rancher looked at the heavens above them, as though he was seeking spiritual guidance in the blue sky.

'It ain't so bad, Gene boy.' Tomahawk gave a toothless smile. 'I ain't so bad with a skillet. I could be the cook for the trail drive.'

Adams looked down at the two figures. 'What? I ain't gonna let you cook for the boys, Tomahawk. Hell. They'll end up poisoned, dead, or they'll quit after the first day.'

Tomahawk blinked. 'That's a leetle bit harsh.'

'Gene's right, you old fool.' Johnny held on to his saddle horn and threw himself on to the back of the pinto pony. 'You can't boil water without

18

burning it. We need a real experienced critter to replace Cookie.'

'We could go to town and have us a look for a cook, Gene boy,' the wily old cowboy suggested. 'Have us a drink while we're there looking.'

Adams stared at the older man. 'You had something to do with this, Tomahawk. You bust his leg somehow.'

Johnny drew the reins up high. 'He's right. We could go to town and try and find us a new cook, Gene.'

Gene Adams continued to breathe heavily as though attempting to blow his frustration out of his body. 'A trail-drive cook is a pretty tough job and not many folks can handle it. They have to survive on a couple of hours' shuteye a day and not only keep the boys fed but tell them when to work and when to rest up. Nope. We ain't likely to find us an experienced cook in town, Johnny.'

Tomahawk clambered up on to his horse. 'Maybe we could find one over in Fargo Springs, Gene boy. I heard that the Circle J has just returned from their drive to McCoy. They gotta have themselves a cook for hire. What ya think?'

Adams turned the mare. He sat staring at the

bluebonnets for a while before answering. 'We were going to set out in two days and now we have to ride for at least two days over to the Circle J. Then if we do find us a cook we have to bring him back and that'll take us another two days.'

Tomahawk shrugged. 'Could be worse.'

'How?' Adams raised an eyebrow.

'Could be a three-day ride, Gene boy.'

Johnny rubbed his jaw. 'So we'll be a few days late. We can always make it up if we get the boys to ride an extra hour or so a day to make up the time.'

Adams frowned. 'I've given my word to the cattle agents up north that we'll have the herd in McCoy by the first of next month. I sure hate running that close to the wire.'

'We sure ain't gonna get no place unless we stops gabbing and starts for Fargo Springs.' Tomahawk turned his black quarter horse and tapped his spurs. The horse galloped off. Tomahawk yelled back at them. 'C'mon.'

Johnny and the rancher swung their horses around and stared through the hoof dust at the wily old-timer as he rode away from them. Both men rose in their stirrups and whipped their reins across their horses' tails. The horses took flight in pursuit.

When Adams's high-shouldered mount drew level with the smaller horseman he looked at the whiskered face. He leaned across the distance between them at his old friend and then shouted at the top of his voice.

'Hey. You ain't told me exactly how Cookie bust his leg, Tomahawk. Did you have anything to do with it?'

Tomahawk spurred harder. He did not answer.

Adams glanced at Johnny as the youngster's pinto pony moved to where the quarter horse had been only seconds before. Both men smiled at one another. 'C'mon, boy. We got us an old goat to catch up with.'

The two Bar 10 riders thundered through the clouds of dust and started to catch up with the wily character. Gene Adams did not like it, but he was headed for Fargo Springs and the Circle J.

The tall grass swayed in the gentle breeze beneath the Texas sun as Adams led his two comrades through the grazing herd of longhorn steers. A line shack stood with three horses tied up to a rail at its side. Adams recognized the mounts as he drew rein beside them, and knew exactly which of his many cowhands belonged in each of their saddles.

The chestnut mare halted. He swung a long leg over his bedroll and dismounted as Tomahawk and Johnny caught up with him. He tossed his reins up to the older horseman.

'You stay here, you old goat,' Adams ordered.

Johnny looked at both men in turn. 'What'll I do?'

'You make sure Tomahawk don't do nothing dangerous.' Adams said, grinning, then stepped up on to the boards outside the cabin door. It opened and the rancher stopped in his tracks. He studied the familiar faces which greeted him.

Rip Calloway, Happy Summers and Red Evans meandered out into the blazing sunshine. They looked at the rancher with a mixture of surprise and concern.

'What ya doing here, Gene?' Happy asked as he ran his tongue across the gummed paper of his cigarette, rolled it between his fingers and then poked it into the corner of his mouth. 'We was about to bring these steers down to the ranch house to mix them in with the others. Ya come to help?'

'Not hardly, Happy,' Adams said drily.

'Then why are ya here?' Red wondered.

'Change of plan, boys,' Adams announced.

Rip plucked his chaps off the hitching rail and wrapped them around his long lean legs. 'I don't like the sound of that, Gene. You never change your plans unless you *gotta* change your plans.'

Adams looked at Red and pointed a gloved finger. 'Ride back to the house, Red. Tell the rest of the hands that we ain't setting out for McCoy the day after tomorrow like we planned. Not until I get us a trail-drive cook.'

'Why'd we need a new cook, Gene. What happened to Cookie?' Rip asked, buckling up his chaps.

'Bust his leg,' Tomahawk piped up.

Adams glanced at the bearded man. 'Shut up, Tomahawk. I still reckon you did something to Cookie.'

Red pulled his reins free of the rail and threw himself on top of his mount. 'Anything else ya want me to tell the crew, Gene?'

'Nope.' The rancher shook his head and watched as the cowboy spurred and galloped away from the line shack in the direction of the distant ranch house. Adams then walked to the door of the shack and stared at the well-fed herd of steers. He had five times as many longhorns spread across the vast Bar 10. These steers were ready for market and any delay in heading out on the drive annoyed the tall man.

'We still gonna take these steers down to the ranch house, Gene?' Happy asked. He struck a match and cupped its flame. He sucked in smoke and then blew at the match.

'Nope,' Adams replied without looking at any of the wranglers around him. 'We're gonna let them get a little fatter eating this sweet grass for a few more days.'

Rip moved closer to Adams. He was one of the few cowboys who was actually taller than the silver-haired rancher, but he had learned many years earlier that it did not pay to look down on Gene Adams. He rested a hip on the hitching rail.

'So you three are headed to Fargo Springs, huh?' Rip asked.

'Nope,' Adams corrected. 'The five of us are headed to Fargo, Rip.'

'It don't take five men to find and hire a cook, Gene.' Rip shrugged as he lifted his gunbelt off the rail and checked his six-shooter.

'It does sometimes, Rip.' Adams glanced at the cowboy.

'How come?' Happy enquired through a cloud of smoke.

'We're going cap in hand to the Circle J.' Adams smiled.

'The Circle J?' Rip repeated.

'Yep. And you know how old Bret Jarvis gets when he sets eyes on me or any of you Bar 10 boys. We're gonna try and hire his trail cook and that'll cost a pretty penny.'

'There's gonna be blood spilled,' Happy said sadly.

'I lost me a tooth last time we bumped into Jarvis and his cowpokes, Gene boy,' Tomahawk said with a sniff.

'You ain't got no teeth.' Johnny laughed.

'Not now.' Tomahawk sighed.

'Safety in numbers.' Rip looked at the rancher. 'Right?'

Adams gave a chuckle. 'Yep. Dead right, Rip.'

THREE

There were a thousand places to hide amid the tree-covered mountains above the sprawling range and sand-coloured rocks that spanned the distance between the remote Los Angelo prison and the town of Fargo Springs. Yet none of the dozen horsemen who rode through the dusty draw beneath the forested mountainside were seeking a place to hide. They had other plans. Plans which their leader had assured them would bring riches beyond their wildest dreams. Each of the riders who followed Cole Logan was expecting their leader to unveil his plans for yet another bank robbery at any moment. The biggest and most lucrative bank robbery any of them had ever undertaken.

The twelve horsemen steered their mounts up a narrow trail until they emerged from a gathering of slim pines at the edge of a high cliff.

Logan eased back on his reins and allowed his mount to rest on the rim of a vast canyon. The outlaw watched the dust from their hoofs float out into the hot air. He then pulled out the box of cigars he had confiscated from the prison warden's office from his saddle-bags. He took one, then handed the box to his right-hand man.

'Share these smokes out, Rem,' Logan said. His sharp teeth bit the end off the long fat cigar. He spat at the ground, then pulled out a match from his vest pocket. 'I got me a feeling that by this time tomorrow we'll be richer than a bunch of kings, boys.'

The outlaws grunted excitedly as they each took a cigar and struck matches. Soon smoke billowed from the eleven desperadoes as they puffed heartily on their cigars.

Logan lighted his own cigar and savoured its flavour as he studied the terrain far below their high vantage point. He was like an eagle considering its prey. A wry smile was etched across his features.

'So which bank are we gonna rob, Cole?' Rem Barker asked eagerly. 'I sure am hankering to do me some bank-robbing. It's sure bin a while.'

There was a heat haze down in the deep canyon but the distant town of Fargo Springs could still be seen beyond a fertile range of grassland. Slowly each of the horsemen noticed that it was not the town that was attracting Logan's attention but something set between the forested canyon and the settlement itself.

'Look yonder.' Another of the outlaws, named Shaky Pete, pointed his cigar at the sprawling settlement beyond the haze and the range. 'There's the town, Rem. That must be where we're headed. Right, Cole?'

'I don't think Cole's looking at the town, Shaky,' Barker noted.

'Nope, I ain't. That ain't where we're headed.' Logan gave a slow shake of his head, then looked towards his men.

Each of the ruthless riders turned to face their leader in total confusion. Barker pulled his cigar from his mouth, turned on his saddle and stared at Logan, who was still looking out at the land below them.

'It ain't?' Barker queried.

Logan nodded. 'Correct. We ain't headed for Fargo Springs to rob us a bank this time, Rem. There's richer pickings to be had far closer than that.'

Barker rubbed his neck and rammed the smouldering cigar back into his mouth. 'But we always rob banks, Cole. We ain't gonna try and hold up a train, are we? I sure ain't got me no hankering to try and rob no train.'

'Me neither,' Shaky Pete agreed. 'Them things are damn dangerous. A man can get himself sliced like bacon if he falls under the wheels of one of them things.'

'Pete's right, Cole.' Another of the outlaws nodded.

Logan looked at his men, then gestured at the land spread out before them. 'Can any of you varmints see any rail tracks down there?'

They all looked. They all shrugged.

'That's coz there ain't none,' Logan snapped. 'We're going to rob a ranch. Simple as that.'

Barker's eyebrows rose. 'What?'

'He said we're gonna rob a ranch,' Shaky Pete repeated.

Barker slapped his hat across the face of the outlaw beside him angrily. 'I heard him, Shaky. The thing is I can't figure out why we're gonna rob a stinking little ranch when there's a town probably full to overflowing with fat banks over yonder.'

Logan rose in his stirrups and pointed at the swaying grass growing over a vast tract of land just beyond the edge of the tree line. 'See it, boys?'

The outlaws all nodded silently.

'That mighty big stretch of grass is slim of steers,' Logan said. 'Right?'

Again his men nodded.

'That's coz they've all been sold,' said Logan. 'Before I got caught by them lawmen a couple of months back I had this job already planned. Lucky for me you busted me free just in time.'

'What job have ya got festering in that head of yours, Cole?' Barker wondered.

Shaky Pete scratched his head and then returned his Stetson back on to his mane of grey hair. 'Ya got me beat, Cole. I ain't got no idea what ya talking about.'

'That stretch of land is the Circle J.' Logan smiled and drew smoke deep into his lungs. 'They're always the first cattle spread in these parts to drive their herd to market up in McCoy. They always get back about this time. No steers but a whole heap of gold coin. They took two thousand white-faced cattle and sold them to the agents from back East.'

'How much money we talking about, Cole?' Barker asked curiously.

'I figure they must have got between ten to twenty dollars a head, Rem,' Logan told him. 'You do the adding up,' he added with a grin.

'Holy cow!' Barker gasped as he looked up from the fingers he was counting. 'That sure is a lot of money, Cole.'

'And a bunch of cowboys ain't no match for us.' Cole Logan gathered up his reins, turned his horse and started down the trail towards the densely tree-filled canyon. 'Just think about it. Bret Jarvis and his Circle J cowhands ain't like a town full of well-armed lawmen. It'll be like taking candy from a baby.'

'Hell. We'll be south of the border before anyone even figures out what we've done, Cole.' Barker swung his mount around and trailed their leader.

'C'mon, boys. We got us a pot of gold to steal,'

Logan called out through a cloud of smoke.

The dozen deadly horsemen continued their journey.

FOUR

The Circle J was always quiet when its cowpunchers returned from a trail drive. Some of its cowboys had already been paid off and had left the cattle spread, but seasoned rancher Bret Jarvis never allowed his best hands to quit. Good wranglers were hard to find and it paid to keep them on the payroll even when most of their stock had been sold at market. Yet the core of his ranch hands now only totalled nine. A bunkhouse set between a barn and Jarvis's long ranch house were at the very centre of the Circle J. In the thirty years of its existence it had never been attacked by anyone.

There had not been any reason for the rancher or any of his hired hands to think that that would ever change. None of them considered that they might one day become a target for a gang of ruthless outlaws.

They were about to be proved wrong.

As the afternoon dust moved across the dry courtyard of the Circle J the rancher and his cowboys were getting ready for their dinner. The aromatic aroma of inch-thick frying steaks filled the air from the cookhouse. The sun was already starting to sink in the sky as it made its daily trip from horizon to distant horizon. Most of the cowboys had finished their chores and were gathering near the stock pens when one of their number noticed the telltale hoof dust filtering from the hillside.

'Hey, Bret,' the cowboy shouted across to the ranch house.

Jarvis came through the wide-open door and made his way down the steps towards his men. He glanced at the group of cowboys and then squinted to where several arms were pointing.

'What ya seen, Clu?' the rancher asked as he drew closer to his men. He rested a hand on the fence poles and rubbed his eyes. 'Damned if I can see a thing. What ya pointing at?'

'Don't ya see it?' the cowboy with far younger

eyes asked his boss. 'We got riders coming down from the canyon.'

Jarvis leaned forward. 'Can ya see that far, boy?'

'He's right, Bret.' Gerry Parks confirmed, nodding. 'We got about ten or more riders headed this way.'

The rancher accepted their word. 'Do ya know them?'

'I ain't seen any of them varmints before,' Clu Sharp said. 'Reckon they must be looking for work.'

Suddenly Bret Jarvis felt a chill trace its way along his backbone. He rubbed his jaw and tried to swallow. He failed: there was no spittle in his mouth.

'I got me a real bad feeling about them varmints, boys,' Jarvis said. His eyes darted to his men. None of them was armed. 'Go get ya gunbelts on. *Now.*'

One by one the cowboys realized that their boss was serious. They could sense his trepidation as the large man pulled his ancient Colt from its holster and checked its chambers. They knew Jarvis never drew his six-shooter unless there was a real good reason.

The Circle J cowboys ran towards the bunkhouse.

FIVE

Dust rose in clouds away from the horses as the outlaws made their way down the steep trail towards the greener pastures and the wooden buildings. Cole Logan held his mount in check as his followers drew level with him. The ground had levelled out a score of yards from the foot of the forested hillside, and the ruthless outlaws knew how to take full advantage of the lush terrain in front of them. Like a cavalry officer Logan raised his left arm and gave a silent signal to his men. It was a signal they all recognized and understood. It was the same silent instruction that Logan had used every time he had led his fearless gang into unsuspecting towns and headed towards the fattest of their banks.

But this was no town with a bank ready for robbing.

This was a cattle spread, with men more used to cowpunching than fending off highly skilled gunfighters. This was going to be a turkey shoot. A bloodbath. A massacre. For months he had planned this day. Even when jailed up and waiting for his neck to be stretched by a rope he had never stopped honing this plan. A plan which now was only a handful of heartbeats away.

A cruel smile filled Logan's unshaven face as he watched the motley crew of naïve cowboys racing back to where their boss still stood. They were innocents: men who wore guns for show but seldom if ever had any reason to use them.

They were cowboys. None of them except Bret Jarvis himself seemed to know anything about the weapons he clung on to.

Out of the corner of his eye Logan could see his riders spreading out in a straight line to either side of his lathered-up horse. A line of heavily armed horsemen would have chilled the resolve of anyone who faced them, but to mere cowboys the sight was terrifying.

Logan gave another silent signal. As their mounts

continued to stride forward the outlaws dragged their rifles from their saddle scabbards and spun them. The sound of each of their Winchesters being cocked for action filled the crisp air.

The outlaws kept their eyes on Logan whilst their mounts thundered on. Months of imprisonment had not had any effect on the determined outlaw leader. He was still the most cunning and dangerous of them all, and they knew it. Logan had the unexplainable ability to know what people would do before they actually did it. He could read people in the same way that some men could read books.

Patiently the horsemen awaited his firm nod, as they had always done. A nod that told them it was time to start shooting.

A time to start killing.

Closer and closer the horsemen rode towards the very middle of the Circle J. The buildings grew larger with each stride of their mounts' long legs. Closer and closer the eyes of the startled cowboys grew bigger until the dozen riders could see the fear in them.

If there had been even a scrap of doubt in the minds of Jarvis and his cowboys of the riders' intentions it evaporated as Cole Logan gave that firm nod of his head.

The shooting started. Not even the most deafening of thunderstorms could have matched the noise of the eleven Winchesters as they erupted into action. Flashes of red venom streaked along the line of riders as their rifles were fired, cocked and fired again. Each of them spurred hard and closed the distance between themselves and their prey. The Devil and his angels of death had come to the Circle J and they had only one aim in mind: to destroy those who stood between them and the gold coin Jarvis had been paid for his herd of white-faced steers.

Clu Sharp spun on his boot heels and crashed into the stock pen in front of them. Blood was spurting from a score of bullet holes in his lifeless body.

The cowboys clawed feverishly at their gun and rifle hammers and vainly tried to return fire. Another volley of deadly lead rang out as bullets left the rifle barrels of the eleven horsemen to either side of Logan. Plumes of gunsmoke were ridden through as the outlaws spurred their mounts harder.

'I'm hit, Bret,' one of the younger cowpunchers

screamed out as he fell on to his knees.

Jarvis gritted his teeth. 'Keep shooting.'

The cowboys tried to obey, but one by one they felt their bodies being punched as bullets found them. His faithful men were falling like flies around him but Jarvis would never quit. He kept firing even as his own large body was knocked back by the outlaws' bullets.

Gerry Parks staggered to the rancher's side. Blood was pouring from half a dozen holes in his body. He tried to talk but then dropped on to his face next to Jarvis's boots. The rancher narrowed his eyes and tried to see only the riders who were still charging towards the centre of the Circle J. He kept firing but there was so much gunsmoke hanging in the dry air that he could no longer see any of their attackers.

Shots ripped into the fence poles behind which Jarvis and his cowboys were standing. Thin whitewashed poles were no protection against lethal lead. A million splinters showered over the rancher and those who remained of his loyal cowboys. The splinters mixed with the acrid gunsmoke and created a pall of blinding dust. It filled the cowboys' eyes and burned like branding-irons.

'I'm out of bullets, Bret,' a pitiful voice piped up to the right of the rancher. Jarvis turned and was about to speak when he saw the kneeling cowboy being thrown backwards after being hit by countless shots.

The rancher rubbed the burning dust from his eyes and then, to his horror, saw the last of his men fall into the dust. A lake of blood covered the ground.

Jarvis cocked his gun again. He was about to turn when suddenly he felt another impact. This time in his left leg. The sound of the bone breaking filled his ears. Jarvis tumbled like a felled tree. The veteran rancher stared in disbelief at his shattered leg. Blood was pumping furiously from the savage wound.

It would be the last thing Bret Jarvis would ever see.

Another volley of shots rang out from Logan's riders' carbines. The rancher's chest burst apart as bullets tore through Jarvis. Every shot hit the prostrate rancher dead centre. Scarlet gore spread like wildfire across the shirt and vest of the rancher as his head crashed back on to the ground.

Every one of the Circle J cowboys lay in a pool of

blood. Blood which spread out across the well-trodden earth. The dozen riders galloped into the very heart of the cattle spread.

The horsemen drew rein above the bodies.

Logan spat at the blood-soaked corpses. The outlaw leader had not even drawn any of his own weapons. There had been no call. His men had been more than capable of dispatching a handful of hapless cowboys. A small twister of dust rose from the hoofs of the outlaws' mounts as each man gloated over his handiwork.

'Damn!' Shaky Pete snorted gleefully. 'I ain't had me as much fun in all my days, boys.'

'Anyone wounded?' Logan yelled out before relighting his cigar.

There arose a chorus of laughter.

'Reckon not,' Logan said through a cloud of smoke.

Barker thrust his smoking rifle back into its scabbard beneath his saddle and dismounted. It took little time for him to satisfy himself that each of the men lying in the pool of blood was dead. He looked up at Logan.

'They're all dead, Cole.'

'Good shooting, boys.' Logan looped a leg over

the neck of his horse and slid to the ground. He tied his reins to one of the smouldering bullet-ridden fence poles and started towards the ranch house. 'Now let's go find where these dumb critters hid their gold coin.'

Barker walked beside their leader. 'Ya figure they got a safe, Cole?'

'Nope,' Logan answered. 'Bet there ain't even a lock on that ranch house door, Rem.'

The outlaws dropped from their saddles and trailed their leader across the yard and up the steps towards the open door of the ranch house. Logan had been correct. There was no lock on the door. The men entered. The room in which they found themselves was far cooler than the yard.

'Where'd ya figure they hid the cattle gold, Cole?' Barker asked a second before Logan stopped beside a rocking-chair.

Logan glanced at his men, then picked up two hefty canvas bags. The sound of jingling coins filled the ranch house. All eyes focused on the bags.

'They didn't hide their money, Rem.' Logan grinned as his right-hand man took one of the heavy bags and looked inside it at the gleaming gold.

'How much do ya figure we got here?' Barker asked, his eyes widening as he took in the sight of the bright coins.

Logan hoisted both bags on to a long table that stood in the centre of the large room. 'Count it and share it out, Rem. Equal shares for all, just like I promised.'

As the hardened outlaws eagerly began to count their loot and stack the gleaming golden coins in twelve piles on the large table Shaky Pete sniffed at the air. 'I smells me steak frying, Cole.'

Curley Jones was one of Logan's men who seldom spoke but even he could not ignore the aromatic aroma which was drifting into the large room from the kitchen beyond.

'That sure smells good,' Curley observed as his well-trained fingers reloaded his Winchester. 'Reckon we arrived just as them useless critters were about to have their supper.'

Cole Logan sat down in the rocking-chair and struck a match along his pants leg. As its flare subsided the ruthless outlaw raised it to the still lengthy cigar. He sucked in smoke, then tossed the match aside. He looked at Shaky Pete and grinned.

'Find it and we'll share that out as well,' Logan

said, smoke trailing from his lips. 'Killing always makes me hungry, Pete.'

SIX

A lone coyote howled out in the blackness. It had been several hours since the blazing sun had set across the range behind them yet none of riders seemed have noticed. They had forged on in defiance of their weariness and the arrival of nightfall. Yet Gene Adams knew that, even though his cowboys would ride until they dropped, their mounts needed rest, water and grain. The rancher stopped his mare. The Bar 10 horsemen eased back on their reins and halted their own mounts beside him at the top of a high ridge. A bright moon illuminated twin mesas which stood like eerie giants a few miles from where the riders rested. Each rocky pillar bathed in the bright yet strange light. Adams stared at the land that lay before them with more than a passing curiosity.

They had been riding since dawn. It was the second day of their long journey to the large cattle spread near Fargo Springs. There were few short rides in Texas. Dust floated up towards the full moon, which hung beneath a cloudless canopy of black velvet. The Bar 10 cowboys were exhausted and sore but none of them would ever have admitted it. It would have been a sign of weakness.

Gene Adams stared out across the wide range without uttering a word to his ranch hands. It was as if he was looking for something but did not know what that something might be. After what seemed like an eternity to the four cowboys Adams tilted his head and looked back at his wranglers.

Adams removed his black hat and beat the trail dust off it against his leg. He looked at the wily old-timer sitting astride his black gelding beside him. 'How long do ya figure it'll be before we reach the Circle J, Tomahawk?'

'I reckon that if we get up at sunrise we'll be there by noon,' Tomahawk answered. Then he realized that Adams had not said 'Fargo Springs' but 'the Circle J'. Tomahawk leaned forward and tugged on his pal's jacket sleeve. 'Hold on a minute there. Ain't we going to Fargo Springs first, Gene boy?'

Adams replaced his hat upon his silver hair, dismounted and sighed heavily. 'Now why the hell would we want to waste time and go there? We sure ain't likely to find us a trail cook in that outhouse of a town. All we'd find there is a bunch of saloon gals and cheap whiskey.'

The older man dropped down beside Adams. 'We could look though. It ain't gonna cost us nothing to take us a look.'

'It'll cost us time, Tomahawk,' Adams corrected.

'Can't we just go and take us a leetle peep, boy?' Tomahawk pressed. 'I reckon it'll be a lot safer than squaring up to the Circle J hands.'

Adams shook his head and pointed at the distant twin mesas. 'There just ain't no call for us to waste time going to Fargo Springs, Tomahawk. The Circle J is closer if we cut up through them mesas yonder.'

Rip lowered himself to the ground and stretched his long frame. Something clicked and the wrangler smiled. 'That's better. My back has bin stiff for the last ten miles.'

Tomahawk followed Adams to where the rancher

was securing his reins to a sapling.

'Hell! I'm thirsty, Gene boy. I ain't had me no whiskey since Easter,' the old-timer grumbled. 'A man gotta have some liquor in his innards. It's in the Good Book.'

Adams removed his canteen from the saddle horn. 'I don't recall nothing about drinking rye in the Bible, ya old buzzard. Besides, you get real troublesome when you're liquored up.'

'That's coz ya never let me have none,' Tomahawk wailed, sniffing like a frustrated child. 'My body goes into shock.'

'I ain't changing my mind,' Adams insisted.

'We might get us a drink at the Circle J, Tomahawk,' Johnny Puma said, jumping down from his saddle. 'If Jarvis don't shoot us I reckon there's a real good chance he might offer us some whiskey.'

'Might?' Tomahawk sniffed. 'I might get kidnapped by a herd of real fancy females, but it ain't hardly likely, ya young whippersnapper.'

Happy dismounted and untied his bedroll laces from behind his saddle cantle. He glanced at Adams as the tall rancher kept looking out at the moonlit land that lay before them. 'Something troubling you, Gene?'

Adams gave a nod. 'Yeah. I'm sure that I heard distant rifle shots a few hours back. Leastways, it sure sounded like rifle fire.'

Johnny glanced at Adams. 'I thought it was thunder.'

Adams pointed at the sky. 'That's what I thought, but look at that sky, Johnny. There ain't even the memory of a cloud up there, so it couldn't have been thunder. The more I think on it the more I'm sure it must have been shooting I heard.'

'Yeah. I think I heard something that sounded a lot like shots earlier.' Happy dropped his bedroll on to the ground, licked his index finger, then raised it above his head to test the direction of the gentle breeze. He nodded to himself. 'Sound carries on the wind and the wind is sure coming from the direction we're heading.'

Adams narrowed his eyes and stared at the moonlit landscape. 'And there's only one thing out there in that direction. The Circle J.'

Johnny dragged his saddle from the back of his pinto and laid it down. 'What you two old roosters talking about? So it was shooting we heard. So what?'

Adams glanced at the youngest of his cowboys. 'So what? Don't you think it's a little strange to hear shooting out here in the middle of nowhere, Johnny? You have to wonder who was shooting and at what.'

'It was probably Apaches or maybe even hunters,' Johnny reasoned as he unlaced his bedroll.

Happy lifted his fender, hooked the stirrup on to his saddle horn and proceeded to untie his cinch straps. 'That shooting sure weren't no hunters, Johnny. It lasted way too long.'

'And there ain't bin an Apache around here for years, Johnny,' Rip added.

Johnny stared off to where the broad-shouldered Adams was still looking. 'And if the noise came from over yonder then it could have only come from the Circle J?'

'Yep. That's what I've been thinking, boy.' Adams nodded his head thoughtfully.

Johnny rubbed his chin. 'It sure was a whole heap of shooting. Way too much shooting.'

The five Bar 10 men brooded on their fear for a moment. The longer they thought about it the more troubled they became. They knew that few shots were ever fired out in the land they travelled through unless someone was in trouble.

Young Johnny Puma rested his wrists on his matched pair of Colt .45s. Unlike most of the cowboys on the Bar 10 he had once been a gun-fighter until Adams had taken him under his wing. He was about to speak when something behind him alerted his youthful instincts.

Johnny spun on his heels and drew his guns. 'Riders!'

Adams and the others moved to his side. The sound of their gun hammers being cocked rang out as they all stared out into the darkness.

'You're right, Johnny boy,' Adams said through gritted teeth. 'We got company.'

'Two of 'em,' Rip said. He held his Colt .45 at hip level, screwed up his eyes and squinted at the pair of horsemen who were approaching at speed.

'Who do ya see?' Tomahawk asked. He pulled his Indian hatchet from his belt and got ready to throw it.

Suddenly a familiar voice rang out from the dark-ness.

'Don't shoot, boys.'

Adams recognized the voice. He eased his gun hammer back and holstered his .45.

'That's Red,' the rancher said.

Johnny took a step forward. 'Who do ya figure he got with him, Gene?'

The rancher did not have to reply. Red Evans and wrangler Larry Drake rode through the brush and drew rein a few yards from where their fellow Bar 10 cowboys were standing.

'Hell. We've bin trying to catch up with you boys for the longest while, Gene,' Larry said. He leapt from his mount, holding on to his reins. 'We was starting to think we'd never catch up with you.'

Adams looked at both riders sternly. 'And what are you cowpokes doing here?'

'We come for the fight,' Red said as he dismounted.

'What fight?' Rip queried.

'The fight between you boys and them Circle J critters,' Larry replied with a grin. 'We weren't gonna miss that. Ain't nothing like a good fight.'

Adams gave an understanding shrug of his shoulders. 'I hope we get a chance to oblige you, Larry. I've got a feeling we might not find anyone to fight, though.'

Both Larry and Red were confused. Rip took them to one side and started to explain, while Gene

Adams silently made his way again to the edge of the ridge and looked out towards the twin mesas. Johnny and Tomahawk stood to either side of him.

'Maybe Larry and Red is right, Gene,' said Tomahawk. He sniffed and then returned his hatchet to his belt. 'Maybe we're letting our imaginations get a leetle bit out of hand. Maybe we is gonna end up having us a real sweet fistfight with Bret and his boys.'

'I'd like to think you're right, old-timer,' Adams said.

'Maybe we didn't hear gunplay, Gene?' Johnny suggested.

'It was gunplay all right.' Adams nodded firmly. 'And it came from the Circle J. There ain't one doubt in my mind about that, Johnny.'

Happy walked to the three men, paused, then pulled out his tobacco pouch from his vest pocket. 'Who do ya figure would be shooting on the Circle J, Gene?'

'Rustlers,' Tomahawk said.

'Since when do rustlers head into a ranch that has just sold most of its steers, you old goat?' scoffed Adams, then he sighed.

'Then why would anyone go there?' Happy

asked, sprinkling tobacco along thin cigarette paper held between his gloved fingers.

Adams suddenly felt a chill trace his backbone. He shuddered and lowered his head. 'Gold coin.'

'What about gold coin?' Tomahawk scratched his beard.

'Bret always insists in being paid in gold coin for his herds,' Adams said, his mind racing. 'It's common knowledge and that means it ain't just honest folks who know that – dishonest varmints also know it. I got me a notion somebody might have tried their hand at relieving him of his cattle money.'

'I don't like the sound of that, Gene,' Happy said. He poked his cigarette into the corner of his mouth.

'Me neither. We gotta go and check it out, Gene,' Johnny urged. 'Might be folks needing our help.'

Gene Adams drew a deep breath. 'I think we could be a little late helping Jarvis and his boys, Johnny. If they were still alive they'd still be shooting, by my reckoning. I know old Bret. He'd only quit once he was dead.'

Johnny gave a knowing nod and turned away. 'Yeah, but we still have to go to the Circle J just in case.'

Adams nodded, patted his young friend's shoulder and turned back to his horse. 'You're right, Johnny. We're going to the Circle J OK. Make no mistake about that. We're going even if we're too late to help Bret and his boys.'

'We heading out for the Circle J now, Gene boy?' Tomahawk asked.

'Not until the horses are taken care of.' Adams looked at his men. 'We're going to water, feed and rest up the horses for a couple of hours, boys. Then after we've had some hot vittles we're riding for the Circle J. Agreed?'

Each of the six Bar 10 cowboys nodded in agreement with the rancher.

'I'll make a fire,' Happy said.

Tomahawk lifted the nearer flap of his saddlebags and pulled out a slab of salt bacon. 'I got me some grub.'

Johnny gathered the reins of their horses together. 'I'll take the horses to that creek down yonder, Gene. I'll fill the canteens while they're drinking their fill.'

Each of the riders of the Bar 10 knew, from years of trail drives, the chores they were expected to do. Gene Adams hauled his saddle from the back of his chestnut mare and dropped it on to the ground. He sat on it and ran a gloved hand thoughtfully across his chin.

Red looked down at the rancher. 'Ya ain't angry with me and Larry are ya, Gene?' he asked.

Adams looked up at the wrangler. 'Why would I be angry with you and Larry, boy?'

The cowboy nervously kicked at the dusty ground. He leaned over until only one man could hear his words.

'The truth is I figured that ya might be riled 'coz we come after you and the boys and didn't stay back on the Bar 10,' Red said sheepishly.

Gene Adams smiled and looked at the lean wrangler. 'You boys did the right thing, Red. I reckon I might just need every one of you if my fears prove to be right. Now quit fretting and go help Johnny with the horses.'

Relieved, Red touched the brim of his hat, gathered up the spare canteens and trailed Johnny down toward the creek.

'We headed for trouble, Gene boy?' Tomahawk asked quietly as he sat down next to the rancher.

'Yep. I reckon we are, Tomahawk.'

SEVEN

The reflections of a myriad stars danced across the surface of the fast-flowing river as the riders of the Bar 10 slowly approached. Spirals of dust rose upward from the hoofs of the seven horsemen's mounts as Adams led his intrepid band of cow-punchers down from the ridge and into the high grass towards the wide waterway. They had rested and eaten and their mounts were all watered and fed but, as the moon and stars cast their eerie illumination across the vast land each of the riders knew that this was not the time to be still riding. This was a time for shuteye. Something was wrong, and every one of the cowboys could sense it.

A solitary coyote kept howling at the large moon

somewhere up on one of the high mesas. It was the most chilling of howls any of the cowboys had ever heard. A siren call that seemed to be drawing them to their eventual destiny. The horsemen slowed their horses as they felt the ground soften beneath their hoofs. The river seemed to be alive as the light of the bright moon and twinkling stars danced across its rippling surface.

Adams was first to stop his mount. The rancher raised himself up in his stirrups and surveyed what faced them with narrowed eyes. He balanced and stared across the water at what lay on the other bank. Two massive mesas rose up, leaving a narrow gulch between their sloping foundations. The coyote continued to howl out its warning. A warning which they would ignore.

'Why'd we stop, Gene?' Red asked. He gathered up his reins in his gloved hands. 'We could cross easy. It ain't deep.'

Adams glanced at the wrangler. 'I always look before I leap, boy. Learn that and you might just live long enough to grow some white hairs on that chin of yours.'

The rancher sat back down and turned to the rest of his men. For a moment he did not speak as he looked at his six companions. They were the best of his ranch hands and he was thankful they were with him. Every sinew in his body told him that they were headed into danger and should quit. But Adams also knew that a curious man never learns the answers to unasked questions by playing safe.

'I don't see anything.' Adams eventually said. 'but if my gut instinct is right there's a herd of raiders across that river someplace.'

'It's still a long way to the Circle J ranch, Gene,' Happy added. 'Might be that all we heard was Bret Jarvis's cowpokes letting off steam after when was paid off after the trail drive.'

Adams gave a slow nod. 'I sure hope you're right, Happy. I ain't hankering for a fight but if you happen to be wrong, I reckon we'll have us a real battle on our hands.'

Johnny rubbed his jaw. 'I'm ready.'

'Me too.' Larry nodded.

Rip gave a yawn. 'Reckon I'm about tuckered but there ain't nothing I like better than a good fight.'

Tomahawk said nothing. His keen eyes kept studying the muddy ground. He turned his black gelding, tapped his spurs and rode away from the others. He steered his mount along the riverbank and studied the moonlit ground close to the water's edge. He stopped fifty yards away from his six pals and stared down like an eagle after it has spotted its prey. He had found what he had been seeking.

'What's Tomahawk doing, Gene?' Johnny asked.

'Tracking, Johnny boy. Tracking,' Adams answered as he watched his oldest friend keenly. He swung his chestnut mare around and rode up next to the old man. The rancher halted his horse, looped his reins around his saddle horn and watched the man who, he believed, was the finest tracker he had ever encountered doing what he did best.

'What you seen, Tomahawk?' Adams asked.

'Hoof tracks, Gene boy.' Tomahawk pointed. 'A whole lot of 'em. Look.'

To Gene Adams it was just a mess of muddy churned-up ground but to Tomahawk it told a story he alone could read and translate. 'Going or coming from the river?'

Tomahawk sat upright and squinted across the river. 'I see about twelve sets of hoof tracks and they is all headed into the river, Gene boy. I figure they cut up between them two mesas yonder and headed into Jarvis's land. I'll bet my beard on it. They sure didn't come back this way, though.'

Adams knew that the land on the other side of the river was the boundary of the Circle J. He thought for a moment and eased closer to the wily old horseman.

'A dozen riders headed into the Circle J?'

'Yep.' Tomahawk eased around and looked down river. 'They come from down there.'

Johnny led the other Bar 10 riders to where the older horsemen rested. They drew rein and sat silently listening to the seasoned pair.

'Now that sure is curious. There's only one thing I know about down there,' Adams said through gritted teeth. 'A prison called Los Angelo. I heard tell that's where they take the rottenest outlaws to hang. None of them ever leaves Los Angelo.'

'Until now, Gene boy,' Tomahawk corrected.

'Yeah. Until now.' Adams shrugged and glanced at the bearded horseman. 'By your reckoning twelve or more of them escaped and for some reason headed straight for Circle J land. That don't make a lot of sense. They could have crossed the border into Mexico far easier than heading up here for the Circle J.'

'That's what they done though,' Tomahawk

insisted. 'Tracks don't lie.'

'So ya figure that a herd of jailbirds come this way and crossed over into Jarvis's spread, Gene?' Happy asked.

Gene Adams gave a slow nod. 'Sure looks that way.'

'That must be the shooting we heard,' Johnny said, and sighed. 'A bunch of stinking convicts must have attacked Jarvis and his boys.'

Adams was thoughtful. 'And I don't give Bret or his cowboys much of a chance against that breed of varmint. They have always been a tough crowd at the Circle J but they ain't no gunfighters.'

'Unlike us.' Johnny grinned.

'Thing is, Johnny,' Adams said, 'we all had us hard times before we became cowboys. Bret and his boys have never done anything except punch steers.'

Tomahawk looked at the heavens. 'It'll be sunup in about an hour or so. We still got us a long ride before we gets to the middle of the Circle J, boys.'

'Then we better quit gabbing and slap rein.' Adams grabbed his long leathers, spun his horse and spurred. The high-shouldered mare galloped into the river. 'C'mon.'

As always the riders of the Bar 10 followed their broad-shouldered boss.

EIGHT

It was still dark as the seven horsemen rode through the canyon between the high-spired peaks that dominated the edge of the Circle J. This was no land for raising steers, Adams thought, as he led his cowboys through the shadows towards their distant goal. But it had proved to be a shrewd business move for Bret Jarvis when he had purchased it, for it allowed the rancher access to the river and an endless supply of water. The sloping sides of the mesas dwindled away on the edge of the grassland as rocky ground became fertile range. The grass was high, as most of the Circle J stock had been driven north to McCoy. Gene Adams knew that his rival would soon have these ranges filled with new stock, or at least he would if he were still alive.

The riders of the Bar 10 could see the heart of the Circle J a few miles ahead of them. The white-washed buildings bathed in moonlight stood out like beacons to the weary cowboys.

'We ought to reach there in another hour or so, Gene,' Tomahawk said as he kept his small gelding moving beside Adams's tall mare. 'We sure made us good time through the canyon.'

'That canyon ain't a place to linger, Tomahawk,' the rancher said. 'A man can get himself bush-whacked in a canyon with sides as high as that.'

'Ya darn tooting,' Tomahawk agreed.

The horsemen spurred. They drew closer to their destination with every beat of their hearts. Soon the mounts were at pace and travelling faster than it was wise to force exhausted horses, but the Bar 10 men sensed that there was a need for urgency in their reaching the moonlit ranch house.

After covering more than half of the distance between themselves and the ranch house and out-buildings their horses began to defy their masters and slow. Adams glanced along the line of riders who flanked his chestnut mare. Each of the cowboys' horses was snorting nervously, just as his own horse was doing.

'Hold up,' Adams called out. 'Something's wrong. The nags are skittish.'

The Bar 10 cowboys stopped their mounts.

Tomahawk fought with his nervous gelding. 'These nags can smell something ahead, Gene boy. Something awful bad.'

'You're dead right, old-timer,' Adams agreed as he screwed up his eyes and strained to see further than the moonlight would allow. 'Damned if I can see anything though. Can any of you boys make out anything in the courtyard over yonder? You've got younger eyes than me.'

'I can see something close to the house, Gene,' Johnny said. He raised a hand and pointed. 'Looks like a bunch of shadows but I can't make out nothing else.'

The rancher sighed and jabbed a finger at the air. 'Anyone see anything moving besides those horses in them corrals between the house and the barn?'

The cowboys shook their heads.

'I sure don't see any men moving around,' Johnny said in reply. 'That is kinda troubling, ain't it?'

'Yeah,' Adams agreed. 'Real troubling.'

'What do ya figure is making these horses so ornery, Gene?' Happy asked as he battled with his buckskin quarter horse. 'I ain't never seen any of them as nervous as they are right now.'

Thoughtfully Adams bit his lower lip. 'Only the stench of death makes well-trained horses this skittish, boy. Horses can smell it better than we can.'

Before any of the cowboys could utter another word a flash lit up the far-off courtyard. No more than a second later the deafening sound of a rifle being fired rang out.

A bullet tore the hat off the silver-haired rancher, sending it flying up into the air.

NINE

The seven riders leapt from their horses into the high grass as one shot after another followed in quick succession. Each of the experienced cowboys held on to his reins firmly as the horses tried to escape the bullets that were streaking through the air. At last the shooting stopped.

'His carbine is empty, Gene,' Johnny Puma called out. He rose to his feet and threw himself back on to his saddle. 'All I gotta do is get to him before he can reload the damn thing.'

Adams stared in disbelief at the youngster. 'Don't be a fool, Johnny.'

Johnny did not listen. He swung the pinto around until it was facing the distant ranch house.

Johnny spurred.

The six other men got up beside their horses and watched as the pinto pony charged across the range towards the building at the centre of the Circle J. Tomahawk grabbed hold of Adams's sleeve and gave it a mighty tug. The rancher looked into his bearded face.

'We gotta stop him, Gene boy,' Tomahawk said. 'Stop him before he gets his head blown off his young shoulders.'

Rip Calloway grabbed his saddle horn and poked a boot into his stirrup. 'Tomahawk's right. I'm riding to help Johnny before he gets himself killed.'

'You're right. Come on, boys,' Adams growled like a bear and drew his mare closer. 'We better try and catch up with that young hothead.'

The six riders from the Bar 10 hastily mounted and spurred their mounts into action. They thundered across the range in pursuit of Johnny Puma.

Johnny stood in his stirrups and lashed the tails of his reins across the black-and-white tail of his mount as it obeyed its master and raced through the eerie moonlight toward the whitewashed poles of the corral. With every long stride of the pinto Johnny could see the shadowy figure behind the fence poles more clearly. The pony thundered towards the place to which its master was steering it. As Johnny closed the distance on the rifleman he saw the gunsmoke lingering above the corral. The pinto kept galloping.

Then the young rider saw the shadowy figure kneeling just inside the corral. The long barrel of a rifle was jutting up from the man's lap as his hands desperately tried to push bullets into its hot magazine.

The figure rose and levelled the Winchester at the charging horse and rider. Johnny dragged rein, pulled his right boot from its stirrup and leapt from his saddle. He flew over the corral poles and caught the shadowy man around the shoulders. A deafening red hot shaft of flame erupted from the rifle barrel as Johnny and the shadowy figure crashed into the ground. They wrestled but it was Johnny who remained on top of the rifleman. The rifle clubbed the Bar 10 cowboy several times across his arms before Johnny angrily tore the weapon from the hands of his foe. Johnny threw the rifle away and forced the man back down against the ground.

A fist came smashing into Johnny's jaw. His head

rocked before he returned the punch with equal accuracy and force.

The man raised a boot and kicked out. Johnny gasped as it caught him in the belly. He refused to be beaten; he grabbed out and gripped the man's bandanna. He jerked the man up with his left hand and landed another ferocious blow into his face. The sound of gloved knuckles finding a chin rang out around the courtyard.

The Bar 10 cowboy then sent another clenched fist into the jaw of the man. He repeated the action again and then felt his opponent go limp. Johnny released his grip on the bandanna and watched as the man's head fell back and hit the ground. With his fists still clenched Johnny stood with a boot to either side of the helpless figure.

'Get up and fight,' Johnny snarled at the unconscious figure sprawled out beneath him.

The rest of the riders of the Bar 10 reached the yard and drew rein beside the pinto. Adams dismounted quickly and raced towards where his youngest cowhand was hovering.

'He's out cold, boy,' Adams said. He clambered through the poles and knelt beside the unconscious man stretched out between Johnny's boots.

Suddenly the face of the rancher changed expression. 'This critter is wounded.'

'We never fired no shots,' Tomahawk said.

Adams inspected the man. 'Somebody put three holes in this critter. Look at him. He's soaked in his own blood.'

Johnny knelt next to the motionless man. 'No wonder he didn't put up much of a fight.'

Gene Adams stood and pointed at his men. 'What you waiting for? Get this critter into the house so we can see if he can be helped.'

Rip, Happy and Larry, as the rancher had ordered, lifted the stricken figure up off the ground and carried him into the dark interior of the house. Adams trailed Johnny up the steps of the ranch house. Tomahawk scampered between them as they paused.

'Tend to our horses, Red,' Adams said to the only one of his men remaining beside the corral posts.

Red gave a slow nod, then pointed a gloved finger to the shadows next to the barn. 'Hey, Gene. Is that what I think it is?'

Adams looked to where his wrangler was indicating. The rancher jumped down to the ground from the veranda and raced across the moonlit sand until he reached the shadows beside the high-roofed barn. He stopped, then turned away. Johnny and Red raced to his side.

'What is it, Gene?' Johnny asked as Red walked slowly up to both men.

'Dead folks, Johnny,' Red said. 'A whole heap of them.'

'Jarvis?' Johnny asked Adams.

Gene Adams gave a solemn nod. 'Yep. It's Bret and a lot of his boys. I can't tell how many, the way they've been piled up.'

Johnny turned and looked back at the ranch house as oil lamps suddenly cast their amber illumination across the yard. He swallowed hard.

'That must be one of the Circle J boys I tangled with, Gene,' he said. 'Hell. I wouldn't have hit him so hard if I'd known.'

Adams sighed. 'You didn't shoot him, Johnny. There was no way for you to figure that he was one of Bret's boys. If he is.'

Red walked with the two men back towards the house. 'Gene's right, Johnny. That might be one of the varmints who killed Jarvis and his hands for all we know.'

Adams patted Red's shoulder. 'Tend the horses,

Red. Me and Johnny will find out who that critter is.'

Red touched the brim of his Stetson and watched as Adams led the younger cowboy up the steps and back into the ranch house.

TEN

The sky had changed from black velvet to an eerie bluish hue as one by one the stars faded and the large moon disappeared. As though some unknown deity had set the heavens aflame an almost blinding light spread across the Texas terrain instantly. Not even the fastest of wildfires could have equalled the speed with which the sunlight raced from the horizon and illuminated everything in its path. Sunrise had once again arrived like quicksilver. It bathed the dozen horsemen in its unforgiving light and more than welcoming heat. The frost which had taken the entire night to spread out across the ground sparkled for a few brief moments and then evaporated in the sunlight.

Outlaw leader Cole Logan led his eleven followers across the range of swaying grass like a triumphant cavalry general after a valiant battle. But there had been no valiant battle, only a depraved massacre of innocents. For all their weaponry the cowboys of the Circle J had stood no chance against ruthless men who had attacked them. For the Logan gang knew how to kill. They were probably the best bank robbers in Texas. They were also the most deadly. Few men who stood up against Logan's hand-picked gang ever survived to tell the tale. They had used their well-rehearsed clearing-of-the-streets technique to dispatch the Circle J cowboys.

The Logan gang's twelve horses had been exhausted before they had reached the Circle J. Now, laden with their equal shares of hefty gold coin, the animals were flagging and slowing with each passing minute while their masters mercilessly spurred them on and on.

As the morning light spread over the belaboured horses, it appeared that only Logan noticed the animals' plight and reasoned that this was not the kind of terrain to travel through on horses that were obviously spent.

Logan noted that his men's mounts were lathered up just like his own horse. It had taken three hours to travel a distance that fresh mounts could have covered in less than one. The outlaw leader drew rein and studied the land that was spread out around them in the early-morning sun. Logan knew that off to their right, no more than five miles away, was the unmarked border with Mexico, a country where he knew they could live like kings with their ill-gotten gains. Logan also realized that the nearest town south of the border was at least twenty miles away. There was little in between, except a desert that was littered with the bleached bones of men and animals that had travelled there unprepared.

The desert took no prisoners. It killed the naïve without mercy, just as his men had killed Bret Jarvis and his Circle J cowhands. Logan could see that none of their horses could cross the desert and reach the safety of the nearest of the Mexican towns.

It did not take a genius to work out that every one of their horses was finished. The sweat-drenched animals hung their heads in exhaustion as the outlaws sat watching their leader.

Yet his honed survival instincts had worked out

the solution to their plight. His only problem was to convince his men. Even though they had always trusted his leadership he wondered how well his solution would sit with them, for they were tired and well-fuelled with the whiskey they had discovered at the Circle J ranch house. Tired men were always hard to reason with. Drunken men were even more difficult. Logan slowly pulled a cigar from his jacket pocket, bit off its tip and rammed it between his teeth. He said nothing as he scratched a match across his saddle horn and cupped its flame. He sucked in smoke and watched as Barker moved his mount next to his own.

'What's wrong, Cole?' Barker asked, draining his canteen of its last drop of water. 'Why'd we stop? Hell. I can see Mexico from here. C'mon. Let's ride. There ain't no posse that'll trail us down there.'

'Change of plan, Rem,' Logan said through a cloud of smoke.

Rem Barker returned his stopper to the neck of his canteen and glared at Logan. 'Change of plan? What ya talking about, Cole? Ya said we was going to Mexico after we took that gold from the Circle J. The longer we hang around here the more likely it is that some butt-brained *hombre* with a taste for glory and the reward money on our heads will start shooting at us.'

Logan waved a weary hand at their mounts. 'These horses are spent, Rem. Look at 'em. We can't get far on these nags and it's a long way to the nearest Mexican town. We need us fresh animals and maybe some pack-mules. I sure don't want to end up hauling gold coin on foot. Do you?'

Barker gritted his teeth. 'I sure don't. Not in them Mexican deserts, anyway.'

The riders were troubled but knew that their leader was right. Logan was always right.

'We should have taken some of them cowboys horses back at that ranch, Cole,' Shaky Pete said. 'Where we gonna find us fresh horses and pack-animals out here?'

Logan adjusted himself on his sweat soaked saddle and pointed his cigar to their left. 'There.'

The outlaws looked to where Logan was indicating.

A dozen sets of eyes focused through the heat haze on the sprawling town of Fargo Springs. One by one they started to smile.

'They not only got plenty of fresh horses for sale,

they also got plenty of saloons and two mighty fine banks.' Logan raised an eyebrow as he saw his men taking in his words. 'We might even add some more money to our tally.'

'We could sure get a lot of whiskey on the back of a couple of pack-mules,' a grinning outlaw thought aloud.

'That's right, Curley,' Logan agreed. 'We can also get a damn lot of money on 'em as well. Just think about it. We're already rich but with bank money added to our tally, we'll be richer than their damn emperor.'

'We'd never have to leave Mexico again, Cole,' Barker said, turning his own horse to face the distant town. 'If we robbed one of them Fargo Springs banks as well I figure we'd be set for life.'

'Which one of them banks are we gonna rob, Cole?' Shaky Pete asked. He bit off a lump of tobacco and started to chew vigorously.

With a satisfied smile Logan looked at his men. It had not been as hard as he had expected to persuade them to accept his new plan of deadly action. Perhaps it was because they had reduced the Circle J cowboys to a bloody memory and had not even suffered a scratch in the process.

'Yeah, which one of them banks are we gonna rob, Cole?' Rem Barker repeated Shaky Pete's question. 'As I recall both of them are pretty sweet. Which one of them will we relieve of its money?'

For a few moments Logan said nothing as he repeatedly filled his lungs with the acrid smoke of the cigar between his teeth. Then his head tilted and he stared into Rem Barker's eyes.

'Which one? Both of 'em, Cole,' Logan confidently answered. '*Both* of them.'

The twelve riders cheered loudly. They had the taste of one bloody victory in their mouths and wanted more of the same. A lot more of the same. Some men had an appetite for killing. An appetite which could never be satisfied.

One by one the outlaws eased their mounts away from the dusty ridge until they were facing the distant town. Logan chewed on his fat cigar and left a trail of smoke hanging on the dry morning air as he encouraged his mount on towards the unsuspecting Fargo Springs. The outlaw leader glanced over his shoulder at the eleven deadly horsemen.

'C'mon, boys,' Logan called out.

They spurred.

ELEVEN

The wounded cowboy lay on the long well-padded couch inside the Circle J ranch house, surrounded by the Bar 10 men. Blood continued to seep from the trio of bullet holes in his lean body as he slowly regained consciousness. He fought with his nightmares and then opened his eyes. For a few seconds his tanned face showed such terror as few men ever experience as he focused on the six men who loomed over him in the rays of the morning sunshine that filtered through the windows of the large room.

Adams took hold of the cowboy's flailing fists and sat on the edge of the long seat. He looked at the bloodstained shirt and pants, then glanced up at Tomahawk.

The cowboy tried to rise but failed. 'Let go of me.'

'Easy, son,' the rancher drawled.

The cowboy stopped trying to fight. He relaxed. 'I know who you are. Ain't you Gene Adams from the Bar 10?'

'Yep.'

The wounded cowboy looked around at the faces that stared down at him. 'Ya brought ya boys with ya.'

Adams leaned closer. 'You got a name?'

'They call me Stonewall.' The cowboy gasped as pain tore through him. He screwed up his eyes and arched in agony. Then he relaxed again and looked into Adams's eyes. 'I was shot. We was all shot by a bunch of stinking riders. They stacked us all in a pile by the barn. They must have figured we was all dead. When I woke I was real surprised. I thought I was dead just like Bret and my pals.'

'Why'd ya shoot at us for?' Johnny asked.

'I thought they had come back,' Stonewall replied drily. 'It was dark and I'd only been awake for a few minutes or so. I seen me a bunch of riders and got scared. I didn't want to end up like the boys.'

'How many were there?' Adams asked.

'Twelve.' Stonewall nodded. 'I counted them before they drew their rifles and started picking us off. Twelve of the meanest-looking bastards I ever set eyes on. They sure could shoot good, though.'

'I was right,' Tomahawk said with a firm nod. 'I said there was twelve of the scum sucking varmints.'

'Mr Adams?' Stonewall took hold of the Bar 10 rancher's jacket sleeve. Adams looked at him.

'What, Stonewall?' Adams asked, trying to ignore the blood which kept flowing from the bullet holes in the cowboy's shirt.

'Am I gonna die?' The cowboy coughed and blood trailed from the corners of his mouth. 'Am I, Mr Adams?'

The cowboys who were standing around the couch turned away from the badly wounded man. Each of them knew the answer to Stonewall's question and were thankful that it was not any of them who were obliged to answer it. Only Tomahawk remained close behind Gene Adams's shoulder, as he had done for four decades.

Never being a man to lie, Adams lowered his head. He stared at his knees and searched for the right words to answer the now frightened young cowboy. He swallowed hard.

'I ain't sure I can answer that, son. I've seen men survive worse but I've also seen men go to their Maker with far fewer bullets in them than you've got. Reckon if we can cut them out you might have a chance but there ain't nothing certain in the life of a cowboy, Stonewall. Nothing except the knowledge that death rides on all of our shoulders, waiting for us to make that one big mistake.'

Tomahawk, standing behind the seated rancher, gave out a long sigh. He placed a bony hand on Adams's shoulder.

'He didn't hear ya, Gene boy,' Tomahawk said in a low whisper.

Gene Adams raised his eyes and looked at the young blood-soaked cowboy lying before him. He was dead. The rancher rose from beside the last of the Circle J cowhands and walked back out into the morning sunlight. Dawn had come and gone without the rancher noticing. Adams paused and rested a hand against a wooden upright. He stared angrily out to where the bodies of Bret Jarvis and his men lay beside the barn. He could see them clearly now. It was not a sight he had ever expected to witness. It sickened and angered him in equal measure.

Tomahawk moved from the interior of the ranch house and came to stand beside the tall rancher. Nobody knew Adams better than the wily old-timer and Tomahawk recognized the fury and sorrow he now saw in his oldest pal. Adams glanced at the bearded figure and gave a nod.

'Ya looks like a stick of dynamite, Gene boy,' Tomahawk remarked. 'I reckon ya fuse has bin lit and you'll explode at any time.'

'You can read me like a book, you old goat,' Adams drawled and stepped down to the courtyard. He paced back towards the barn in well-measured strides. Tomahawk kept up with Adams even though it took twice as many strides of his shorter legs. 'You always could.'

'Ya hurting, son.' Tomahawk sniffed as the sickening fragrance of death greeted their nostrils. 'I've known ya too long not to know when ya dander is up. I know that ya never could tolerate innocent folks being gunned down.'

Adams stopped. 'What's going on, Tomahawk?'

'Damned if I know.'

The rancher rested his hands on his holstered guns and tried to think of a reason for the events that had suddenly overtaken them. It was impossible.

Only madmen could understand senseless slaying. No sane soul could ever do anything but try and clean up the mess.

'What we gonna do now, Gene boy?' Tomahawk scratched his beard. 'We only come here looking for a cook to hire. Damned if I know how we ended up riding into this.'

'But we did, Tomahawk,' Adams said. 'We rode into one mighty bad situation and by my figuring it's up to us to make it right.'

'Why us?'

'There ain't nobody else, Tomahawk.'

The older man screwed up his eyes. He no longer wanted to focus on the horrific vision before him. 'What ya figure we oughta do, Gene boy?'

'Simple, you old goat. We find the varmints that did this and make them pay,' the rancher answered, and turned towards the barn. He walked to its great doors and dragged them open. 'First I'm gonna find a shovel and bury these pitiful boys before the sun starts cooking them.'

Tomahawk shuffled his feet.

'Are ya sure we can find the varmints that done this?' The old man looked at his determined friend. 'There's gotta be more than a hundred directions they could have taken with Bret's gold. They might even be in Mexico by now.'

The rancher looked at the old-timer. He seemed to shrink with the coming of every new season.

'Tomahawk, listen up. With you tracking them we'll find the animals that slaughtered Bret and his boys.' Adams nodded firmly and pointed a gloved finger. 'Nobody can follow a trail better than you. Right?'

'Ya darn tooting. Good thinking, Gene boy.' Tomahawk gave a toothless smile and followed Adams into the barn. 'Them stinking killers don't know who they're tangling with, do they? They ain't got no idea that the bestest darn tracker in the whole of Texas has their scent in his nose, and I'm harder to shake off than a whole pack of hound dogs.'

'Who you talking about again, Tomahawk?' Adams raised an eyebrow. 'Who smells like a pack of old hound dogs?'

'Me!' Tomahawk trailed his friend. 'They'd be quivering in their boots if'n they knew the riders of the Bar 10 was hunting 'em down. Ain't that right, boy?'

Adams found two shovels and tossed one to

Tomahawk. His eyes narrowed and his teeth gritted. He nodded.

'Damn right, Tomahawk. Damn right.'

TWELVE

Fargo Springs owed its very survival to its situation just beyond the boundary of the famed and prosperous Circle J ranch. Over more than two decades it had grown larger and larger as it lived off the fruits of Bret Jarvis's labours. The wealthier the Circle J had become the more prosperity the town had enjoyed. Fargo Springs was like a parasite living off Jarvis and his cowhands. Unlike the Bar 10, which bred the best longhorn steers in Texas, the Circle J had concentrated on white-faced cattle. Both ranches had grown rich as they supplied the insatiable appetites of those who lived back East.

Unlike so many other towns in the West there had never been any real trouble in the sprawling settlement, apart from the usual kind: the same kind as afflicted all similar settlements throughout the West. Wild women, hard liquor and card sharps always tended to create tension as they fought one another for the honest, hard-earned dollars that eventually filtered from the pockets of hard-working cowboys.

But soon they would discover what real trouble was. A kind of trouble none of the folks in Fargo Springs had ever experienced before.

A band of ruthless bank robbers who never showed anyone any mercy was headed into their town. The riders who were closing in on the remote Texan town were unlike the troublesome cowboys they were used to. These were not young hotheads desperate to spend their wages and have a good time. The Logan gang were cut from a cloth utterly different from any fabric the townsfolk of Fargo Springs had ever encountered before.

It was a cloth woven by the Devil himself.

Fargo Springs' main street boasted two juicy, well-fattened banks. They had prospered ever since Bret Jarvis had started to breed his famed white-faced steers and sell them to the Eastern cattle agents. Every business along the well-maintained street owed its existence to the nearby cattle ranch.

Suddenly, one by one, the town's early risers spotted dust drifting heavenward from the trail that was only ever used by the Circle J cowhands. Men, women and children alike began to wave to the horsemen riding towards them. They all had the same thought: Bret Jarvis and his boys were coming to Fargo Springs to spend some of their gold. It was like the Fourth of July whenever the Circle J returned from McCoy after selling a herd.

But the twelve riders who broke clear of the dust were not the riders any of the town's inhabitants were expecting. Cole Logan rode at the head of his followers and squinted towards the innocent people who were waving at them.

Logan looked at Barker and smirked.

'Reckon this will be a whole lot easier than we thought it would be, Rem,' the outlaw leader remarked. 'Look at them. They're waving at us like we were long-lost friends. This will be even easier pickings than the ranch was.'

Barker grinned from ear to ear. 'Reckon so, Cole. I sure reckon so.'

The Logan gang spurred hard. Their mounts tore across the distance between themselves and the town. The closer the horsemen came to Fargo Springs the more the onlookers stopped waving and smiling.

It soon became obvious that none of the twelve riders were Circle J men. None of the dust-caked faces were known to any of the townsfolk, who studied them as they thundered between the outlying buildings and continued on through the wide streets towards the largest of the settlement's buildings.

The livery stable stood alone between two fenced areas of grassland. A score of saddle horses roamed around in one of the pastures. They were well nourished and exactly what Cole Logan sought.

Logan and his cronies drew rein as they reached the wide-open double doors of the tall building. The outlaws dismounted swiftly, except for Logan himself. He remained seated on his spent mount, watching those who were watching his men and himself.

Rem Barker held on to his horse's bridle and looked up at their leader curiously.

'What's wrong, Cole?'

'Nothing, Rem,' Logan responded. Then he eased himself off his sweat-soaked saddle and lowered himself to the ground.

'What ya looking at then?' Shaky Pete asked.

Logan tossed his reins into Barker's hands. 'The town's changed since we were here last year.'

The outlaws looked around them. They could not see any difference in the town's layout, but they knew that, unlike most men, Logan had an incredible memory. If he said something had changed then it was a certainty that it had changed.

Barker rubbed his sweaty brow across his sleeve and edged closer to Logan. 'How has it changed, Cole?'

'The streets ain't the same as they were,' Logan replied.

'Ya dead right, mister.' A gruff voice piped up from the shadows of the livery stable. A dozen sets of eyes darted to where the voice had come from. They watched a large muscular figure move slowly out into the bright sunshine. 'It's changed one hell of a lot. Ya must be mighty observant.'

Logan looked at the stableman. He touched the brim of his hat and smiled. 'Some folks say I am.'

The livery stableman rested a powerful hand against one of the tall doors and paused. 'The town council decided to pull down a couple of streets and build a handful of new houses yonder. Had to alter half the streets in town to make it all fit together again. Damn waste of money and time if'n ya ask me, but I didn't have no vote.'

Logan was concerned. He had the layout of the town as he had last seen it etched into his mind. Every street, alley and short cut was branded into his devilish mind, and now it was all different. He walked up to the man who seemed to stand more than six inches taller than any of his men.

'Why'd they do it?'

'Progress they called it, mister,' the livery man replied with a shrug. 'I sure don't see how Fargo Springs is a better place than it was before. Reckon some of them council folks made themselves a profit on it though. They always do.'

Barker leaned close to Logan. He could see the concern in the face he knew so well. 'What's wrong, Cole? Does it matter that the streets ain't the same as they were?'

Cole Logan raised an eyebrow.

'It might, Rem. It just might.'

The muscular stableman scratched his whiskers and looked at the array of exhausted horseflesh, then returned his gaze to Logan. 'What's ya business with me? Ya want me to look after these nags for a few days until they're up to full strength again?'

'Nope,' Logan said, and aimed a finger at the field of horses. 'I want to buy every one of those horses you got in there.'

'All of them?' the large man asked.

'Yep.' Logan nodded. 'I'll pay top dollar. Gold coin.'

The liveryman was impressed. 'The trouble is them nags is all I got. What if someone wants to buy a horse from me after ya gone?'

Barker pointed at their own horses. 'Sell them our old nags, friend. Like ya said, they'll be fine in a few days once they've rested up.'

Logan was thoughtful. Since entering Fargo Springs they had not seen another horse, apart from those in the livery stable corral.

'Does anyone in town own a horse?' Logan watched the big greasy man beside them. 'I ain't seen any apart from the ones you got fenced up there.'

'Nope.' The liveryman shrugged. 'Ain't no call for any of them to own horses. Besides, most of the critters wouldn't know which end of a nag to feed, let alone manage to haul their sorry backsides up on to a saddle. Even the sheriff don't own one. They never goes anywhere so they don't need horses. If they do have to go someplace they rents a nag from me.'

'So the only other horses in all of Fargo Springs are right there?' Logan was starting to smile again.

'Yep.'

Barker looked at Logan and then at their lathered up mounts. 'I just had me a thought, Cole. If we buy up all the fresh horseflesh and ride south, the only horses left for a posse are ours. And they ain't got more than a few miles of hard riding left in them.'

Logan turned square on the liveryman. 'Name ya price and we'll buy every one of your horses. I'll also pay top dollar for new blankets and livery. Ours are a tad sweat-soaked, as ya can see.'

The brawny liveryman offered a hand to Logan. 'My names Moose Morgan and I sure like the way ya do business. What are you and ya pals intending on doing?'

Logan shook the hand. 'If ya knew ya might need killing, Moose. I'd hate to be forced to kill such a fine specimen as you.'

Moose Morgan grinned. 'Bank robbers?'

The outlaws' faces suddenly went grim. Barker lowered his head and stared at Morgan. 'Why'd ya ask that?'

'I read me dime novels. A whole heap of them.' Morgan took the reins of the nearest horses and led them into the dark interior of the huge building. 'I've bin hoping for years that something exciting like that would happen here, but never thought it would. I hope ya cleans them banks of every damn cent they got.'

Logan watched as the man handled the horses with incredible strength. 'Ya don't seem to be troubled by the fact that me and my boys intend doing exactly that. We intend stripping both banks clean.'

Morgan glanced at Logan as he swiftly hauled saddles from horses and dumped them in the sunlight to dry. He gave a grunt which was half laughter and half anger. He rested and stared at Logan.

'Strip them clean, mister. Them fancy bankers never let me even have an account. They don't like the smell of hard work in their fancy banks. Nope. It ain't gonna hurt me if they ends up broke. I got all my money in an old empty peach jar in the rafters.'

Cole Logan nodded. 'You'll be the richest varmint in Fargo Springs before sundown, Moose.'

THIRTEEN

The seven riders of the Bar 10 rode with revenge brewing in their souls. They thundered like knights on a holy crusade after the dozen outlaws. With the skilful tracker Tomahawk riding point the horsemen knew that it was only a matter of time before they caught up with their prey.

The dust rose into the cloudless blue sky as Tomahawk stopped his quarter horse and surveyed the ground before them. The wily old-timer dismounted as his six fellow cowboys held their mounts in check around him.

Adams watched Tomahawk kneel and run a hand across the surface of the well-used trail. The rancher leaned over from his high perch atop his chestnut mare.

'What is it, Tomahawk?'

Tomahawk was silent for a few moments as he assessed the signs, which only he was skilled enough to understand. At last he rose up and shook his head, as if he did not believe what the clues he had read in the dust indicated.

'These hoof tracks are real deep, Gene boy,' Tomahawk explained. 'I figure they must have shared out the gold between 'em before they left the Circle J. Their horses were already making deep tracks before they reached the ranch. I reckon they got themselves more weapons on their saddles than we ever dreamed about.'

'What difference does that make, old-timer?' Adams pressed. 'So they happen to be loaded for bear? We already figured that much.'

'It means that every one of their horses is plumb tuckered out, Gene boy. That's what difference it makes.' Tomahawk rubbed his bushy beard. 'Now smart folks would have used a couple of packhorses to take the burden. These locobeans have managed to bring their saddle horses almost to their knees. I can't see one of them sets of tracks that ain't swaying like a drunken sailor.'

Johnny swung his pinto pony around and stared at Tomahawk as the old rider clambered back up on to his gelding.

'That means their mounts are gonna start dropping from exhaustion real soon, Tomahawk,' Johnny said. 'Am I right?'

Tomahawk gathered his reins up and looked at his fellow horsemen. 'Ya would be right, Johnny, if'n they'd headed south of the border like we figured they would. Reckon they couldn't have gone more than two miles before their horses began to drop.'

'I figure we'll set eyes on them darn soon, boys,' Larry Drake said. 'I'm ready for a fight.'

'Me too,' Rip agreed.

Adams looked at his six cowhands like a father studies his sons and raised a gloved hand. This silenced them, and Adams moved his mare to stand in front of Tomahawk's black gelding. The eyes of the men locked.

'Finish what you were saying, you old goat. I've known you way too long not to have heard something in that voice of yours that made the hairs on my neck rise. Finish telling us what you read in them tracks.'

Tomahawk nodded. 'Like I said, if'n they'd ridden south we'd be catching up with them real soon, Gene boy. Trouble is they didn't head south at all like we figured.'

Happy struck a match across his saddle horn and cupped its flame to the end of his cigarette. He sucked smoke deep into his lungs and then exhaled.

'Are ya telling us they headed someplace else, Tomahawk?'

'Where?' Red Evans asked, looking all around them. 'There ain't nowhere to ride except down into Mexico.'

Adams straightened up on his saddle. 'Wrong. There is one place those varmints could have headed for. Fargo Springs.'

Johnny rode to come beside the rancher. 'Would they risk it? If they got paper on them and bounty, that sure seems a mighty dangerous place to go.'

Adams gritted his teeth. 'We ain't talking about a bunch of saddle tramps here, Johnny. Whoever these critters are they come from the prison at Los Angelo. I'm figuring they're a lot more dangerous than the usual drifters who ride these parts. If anyone is in danger when they ride into Fargo

Springs it sure ain't them.'

The youngster was about to speak again when suddenly a volley of shots rang out from high up on the canyon walls to their left. Adams felt the heat of a bullet as it passed within inches of his face. Then to his horror he saw Red fall limply from his saddle and crash into the ungiving sand.

More deafening shots echoed out.

FOURTEEN

Shafts of lethal venom came splintering through the sunlight from ledges set high in the ridge above the trail. Over and over again the bullets blasted from unseen rifle barrels and sought the riders below their high vantage point. Red was already lying on the ground as Gene Adams defied his six decades of existence and leapt from his saddle. As the rancher rolled across the ground towards the foot of the sand coloured rockface he heard another of his men yell out in pain behind him.

Adams reached the rugged wall and drew both his guns. His gloved thumbs clawed both their hammers back until they fully locked. He turned, aimed upward and fired both .45s before throwing his back against the wall of rock and cocking the guns again. He screwed up his eyes and stared at the scene before him as the seven horses pounded their hoofs into the ground whilst the remaining cowpunchers swiftly emulated their boss and leapt to the ground.

The air stank of gunsmoke. It was a smell Adams knew only too well. An acrid aroma, which was only worsted by the sickening stench of death.

Adams tried to see which of his boys had been hit besides Red but it was impossible. As their guns blasted in reply the trail became filled with a toxic mixture of gunsmoke and kicked-up dust.

The horses galloped back up the trail behind them as Rip and Johnny hauled Red to where Adams knelt. The rancher glanced at the blood covering the cowboy, then fired his guns again up to where the relentless rifle fire was coming from.

'Is he alive?' Adams growled as he cocked his Colts again.

'Can't tell, Gene,' Rip answered.

'He's out cold,' Johnny added. Then he drew one of his weapons and tugged its hammer back.

Adams looked out to where most of the bullets were being aimed. The dust kicked up as lead ball hit rock. It was like watching a series of lightning bolts.

'Where's Tomahawk?' he suddenly snapped as he vainly tried to see through the cloud of dust and smoke. 'Where is he?'

Then Larry Drake emerged from the wall of dust with his gun firing upwards in time with his long strides. He raced to stand beside his fellow cow-punchers, then dropped down. He shook the spent casings from his smoking gun and clawed for bullets from his belt.

'Who the hell is shooting at us, Gene?' Larry spat.

Adams did not answer Larry's question. He posed one of his own as he thrust one of his six-shooters back into its holster and dragged at the cowboy's collar.

'Where's Tomahawk, Larry?'

Larry gulped hard as he saw the angry desperation in the rancher's face. He shrugged. 'I didn't see him, Gene. All I seen was our horses rearing and the bullets coming down like rain.'

Adams released his grip on Larry's shirt. His eyes darted to Rip and then Johnny. 'Did either of you see him?'

Both cowhands shook their heads silently.

'Damn it all.' Adams swung on his knee until he was facing the level trail again. 'Where is that old goat?'

'I reckon I heard someone call out just as I dismounted to help Red, Gene,' Rip said. He drew one of his guns and quickly fired upward. 'Damned if I could tell who it was that got hit, though.'

'I heard that cry as well, *amigo*.' Adams said. 'Couldn't make out who it came from, though. Pain don't sound like voices.'

Johnny rose up to his full height. 'Hold on a minute there, boys. All this talk about Tomahawk and I just figured that we ain't seen Happy either since the shooting started.'

Gene Adams stood next to Johnny. 'Look out there, Johnny. Can your young eyes see either of them? I sure can't make out nothing but dust.'

Johnny focused hard. He was about to answer when his far more youthful eyes did manage to make out something through the dust and swirling gunsmoke.

'Damn!' he uttered.

'What?' Adams grabbed hold of Johnny's arm.

'I see someone down.' Johnny responded and

then instantly corrected himself. 'No, wait. I see two of them down, Gene.'

More rifle shots tore through the air and pounded into the ground. Adams looked at Johnny. There was urgency in his every facial muscle as he gave the cowboy orders.

'Get up there, Johnny,' Adams told his pal. 'Get up there and stop them *hombres* killing us.'

Johnny gave a firm nod. 'You got it, Gene.'

Rip moved to the rancher's side as Johnny disappeared into the dust beside the steep rockface. 'Where's Johnny gone?'

Adams did not reply as he hastily reloaded both his hot guns. He looked up at the tallest of his Bar 10 cowboys after holstering one of the weapons.

'You reckon you can run with me across that sand to where Tomahawk and Happy are, Rip boy?' Adams asked. 'We might get ourselves killed but if we leave them out there it's only a matter of time before those riflemen finish them off.'

Rip inhaled long and deep. 'Lead the way, boss.'

Gene Adams gave the wrangler a thankful smile. Then his expression changed again. 'You run and I'll follow, Rip. I'll do the shooting at them bushwhackers and you concentrate on getting Happy back to safety.'

'What about Tomahawk?' Rip asked as he readied himself to dash out towards their fallen comrades.

'I'll pluck Tomahawk up.' Adams pointed at Larry. 'You give us cover, Larry. Fire every damn bullet you got up at them rifles. Use Red's guns as well as your own. Savvy? I want those riflemen eating bullets.'

Larry gave a nod. 'You've got cover, Gene. I'll make sure them back-shooters don't poke their heads over that rim long enough to take aim.'

'Good enough.' Adams turned and stood beside Rip. 'You start and I'll follow, son.'

Within a heartbeat Rip and Adams had raced from the rocks out into the churned-up dust as bullets came seeking them from high above. As Adams ran behind the younger wrangler he turned, cocked his gun and fired over and over again. With each shot the rancher sent up towards the hidden riflemen he saw Larry fanning his gun hammer at the same target. Bullets ricocheted all around the riflemen, forcing them to keep their heads low for fear of having them shot off their shoulders.

The Bar 10 men reached Tomahawk and Happy

and went about hauling them off the sand. Sand was kicked up all around them as bullets rained down on them again. At the foot of the wall of rock Larry switched his empty gun for Red's fully loaded ones and blasted them both at the rifles. One of the long-barrelled Winchesters was torn from the grip of one of the unseen riflemen. It flew upward and then came clattering down to where the cowboy stood.

'It don't pay to rile the Bar 10,' Larry shouted as he continued to fire. 'Eat lead.'

Adams dragged Tomahawk off the ground and on to his broad left shoulder. With the skinny old-timer balanced against his neck Adams holstered one gun and drew the other. He dragged back on its hammer. The sound of the gun locking filled the area. Mustering every scrap of his strength Rip managed to hoist the unconscious Happy over his shoulder.

'Ready, Rip?' Adams shouted out above the noise of the constant gunfire. 'You ready to run?'

'Yep,' Rip shouted back.

'Then run, boy,' Adams screamed out. 'Run for your life.'

FIFTEEN

The sound of fevered shooting was below the young Johnny Puma as he ascended the slope up to where the bushwhackers had secreted themselves and also above him. The blazing sunshine seemed to be burning the flesh from his face as he gradually closed the distance on the men, who were still firing down at his trapped comrades. Johnny knew it was up to him to stop them from killing the men he considered closer than kinfolk. Stop them permanently if that was what it took.

The climb up to where the riflemen were hidden was not as hard as some Johnny had attempted in his life, but it was probably the most important.

He moved as swiftly as was possible with his pair

of matched Colts resting in their hand-tooled holsters. Few men could outdraw the young cowboy, who had once been a gunfighter, and he had never feared anyone who faced him. This was a climb more dangerous than any he had previously undertaken, for at any time during his steady trek upward, Johnny realized, one or more of the riflemen might suddenly appear from behind a boulder and start firing.

There was little cover on the crumbling surface of the sand-coloured rock. There was nowhere to hide and survival would depend upon who could squeeze their triggers first.

The last seven feet of the climb would prove to be the toughest. A wall of vertical stone taller than the cowboy himself faced Johnny. This was not a pathway. This was a canyon wall that even the most agile of goats would have found hard to negotiate. Johnny took in as much dusty air as his lungs could manage before he stretched up and gripped the top of the rocky rim. He gritted his teeth, then raised a knee. He poked his boot toe into the soft rock and forced himself up. He repeated the action with his other pointed boot and clung on. He glanced down through the gap between his flat

114

belly and the rocks. It was a long way down across rugged, unyielding terrain to the floor of the canyon trail. This was no place to fall, he thought. Not without getting crippled.

His gloved fingers clawed at the dusty rocks above him and at last he managed to find a stable hold. Johnny then mustered every scrap of his youthful strength and forced himself upward until his head cleared the lip of the rim. All of his muscles screamed for him to stop and lower himself down again, but that was not an option for the cowboy. Gene Adams had charged him with this job. Johnny knew that he was the only one of the Bar 10 cowboys who had a chance of achieving what had to be done.

He squinted into the blinding sunshine, which glared off the near-white dusty surface in front of him, as though from the brightest of mirrors.

The ground was virtually level over the edge of the stony ridge surface. The shooting was now louder and Johnny could see why. The bushwhackers were just beyond four lathered up horses. For a few moments the cowboy did not move from his precarious perch. He felt sure the well hidden gunmen would sense his presence at any moment.

Johnny was wrong. As they continued to fire down into the canyon not one of them even looked over his shoulder. They had no idea that they were no longer alone.

Dust drifted from all around him as he silently eased his whole body on to the safety of the flat ridge. He crawled across it until he was behind the legs of the four tethered horses. Johnny suddenly realized that even if the four gunmen all turned at the same moment and started shooting at him, it would be their horses who were cut down by their lethal lead, long before any of their bullets found him. Johnny forced himself up to his full height. Only then did he notice the distinctive brand shared by all four of the sweat-lathered horses. He ran a glove across the soaplike sweat that covered the shoulder of the nearest of the mounts. The brand was simple.

L.A.P.

'Los Angelo Prison.' Johnny whispered the initials, then looked at the hunched shoulders of the riflemen who were still firing their Winchesters and handguns down into the sun baked canyon. 'They must have stolen these nags when they attacked the prison. Gene and Tomahawk were right. These no-goods are from the prison. I just wonder where the rest of the stinking varmints are.'

A fury swept though the cowboy.

He slowly drew both his guns from their holsters. His thumbs pulled back on the hammers. They clicked into position.

Johnny Puma moved in front of the horses. He was ready. Ready to kill.

The horses did not shy away from the man who had the scent of other horses on him.

Four men were crouched just below Johnny. Three had rifles and the fourth a handgun. They were all shooting down at his pals. The sound of the shooting had been Johnny's only guidance to this place.

It had drawn him like a moth to a naked flame.

He trained his barrels on the four bushwhackers. Every inch of Johnny wanted to kill them. Luckily for them he was no back-shooter.

Johnny squeezed both his triggers. Hot deafening flames shot from the barrels of his .45s. He watched as two of the men's Stetsons were torn from their heads. All four men cried out in confusion. Johnny fired his guns again and removed the hats from the heads of the other two startled gunmen. He shook both Colts and hauled their hammers back again.

'Drop them weapons. Make no mistake, I'll surely kill ya all,' the young cowboy shouted at the top of his lungs. 'You heard me. Drop them weapons. Now.'

The four men stared through the gunsmoke at the lean cowboy with the smoking Colts in his gloved hands. None of them had any doubt in his soul that the youngster meant every word he had shouted.

One by one they dropped their rifles and guns and rose to their feet. They faced the cowboy as Johnny slowly walked towards them.

'Who are ya?' one of the men demanded.

'The question is how come you bastards started shooting at me and my friends?' Johnny yelled back. 'I ain't never liked bushwhackers and ya darn lucky I didn't kill you the way ya tried to kill us.'

'What do ya expect after ya broke Cole Logan out of prison and killed more than a dozen guards and prisoners?' one of the men railed.

Johnny stopped in his tracks. 'We never did that. Who in tarnation are you, anyway?'

'We're guards from Los Angelo,' one of the men

replied angrily, pointing at the Bar 10 cowboy. 'We've bin hunting you ruthless outlaws since you blew up the prison and broke Logan out.'

Johnny stepped forward. 'Guards?'

'Damn right,' another of the men snarled and pulled his coat open to reveal a badge. 'We're only alive coz we were away from the prison getting supplies. When we returned we discovered what you boys had done. We've bin tracking you ever since.'

Johnny tilted his head. 'Then ya ain't much good at tracking, friend. We're from the Bar 10. We're on the trail of the varmints who killed the Circle J cowhands back a few miles. I reckon we must all be after the same vermin.'

The men suddenly looked guilty.

'Ya mean we opened up on a bunch of innocent cowboys?' one of them asked. 'Oh, sweet Lord.'

'We must have crossed trails somewhere,' another of them reasoned. 'We must have mixed your tracks up with those of the gang that fled from Los Angelo.'

'Yep. Ya got kinda confused,' Johnny snarled, his fingers stroking the ice-cold triggers of his guns. 'Just coz none of ya can track worth a damn, I got pals down yonder who are wounded and might be dead.'

The guards looked at each other. They searched for answers in one another's faces but found none. The oldest-looking of them swallowed hard and gestured to Johnny.

'We never meant to shoot innocent cowboys.'

'But ya did,' Johnny spat angrily.

The prison guards looked as sick as Johnny felt. Not one of them could look the cowboy in the eyes. They had made the same mistake that many men who live by the gun tended to do eventually, if they lived long enough. They had put two and two together and made five.

'Ya said ya from the Bar 10,' the shortest of the guards said. 'I've heard a lot about that ranch. How come ya so far away from home?'

'It all started with a busted leg,' Johnny said. He did not add anything more to the statement. Reluctantly Johnny poked his guns back into their holsters but did not secure their hammers with the small safety loops. The young cowboy had not yet decided that this brief showdown was over. He raised a finger and pointed at them all in turn.

'What about our weapons?' a guard asked.

'Leave 'em be,' Johnny snapped.

'We might need them.'

Johnny inhaled deeply. His eyes narrowed. 'Listen up. If any of my pals are dead down in the canyon below, I'll kill you all. Make no mistake about it. I'll kill every damn one of you.'

'Is that a threat?'

'Nope.' Johnny snorted. 'That's a promise. A Bar 10 promise, *amigo*.'

There was something in the tone of the young cowboy's voice that told the prison guards that Johnny Puma meant every word that he had uttered.

'C'mon. You better follow me down to the canyon,' Johnny said. 'Get ya damn horses and follow me.'

'What if we don't care to follow ya?' the oldest of the prison guards asked.

'I'd not take that risk if I was you,' Johnny shouted.

The Bar 10 cowboy started down the slope back towards the canyon. The prison guards followed him with their horses in tow.

None of them spoke again. None of them dared.

SIXTEEN

The dozen outlaws sat astride their fresh mounts with their packhorses tied securely to their saddle fenders and began the slow ride through the afternoon sun into the heart of the sprawling settlement. Cole Logan rode at their head and continued to study every street and alleyway intently. So much had changed since he had last been in Fargo Springs. So many streets were no longer as he recalled them. So many streets had simply vanished and others had sprung up and replaced them. The entire layout of the main thoroughfare had altered beyond recognition. It troubled the leader of the Logan gang far more than he would ever have admitted. For Logan was a man who planned everything in minute detail and kept the blueprints of it all stored inside his festering skull.

It looked as though the town council had hired themselves a pretty good architect in Logan's absence.

As the twelve horsemen rode closer to the heart of the town Logan attempted to replace the original map of Fargo Springs carved into his memory with the new layout. It was not the way he liked to work. Every short cut away from the banks on Main Street seemed to have gone. Logan sucked on a fat cigar and attempted to find substitutes. It was not easy.

He reined back and stopped his horse. His eleven disciples halted their mounts around the brooding, thoughtful Logan as he puffed on smoke and carefully studied the sunbaked street.

'This is Main Street, boys,' Logan said. 'And there are the two banks.'

Shaky Pete shook his head. 'This ain't the way I recalls it, Cole. I got me a bad feeling in my craw about this.'

'Me too,' Curley said, and nodded as others joined in. 'There was a sheriff's office right there and it's gone. Where the hell is the lawman?'

'He might have himself a new one someplace,'

Shaky added. 'One full of well-armed deputies.'

Rem Barker eased his horse next to his leader. He knew that Logan was troubled. 'Ya figure this job is gonna be as easy as ya figured, Cole? Maybe we ought to just fill our packs with liquor and provisions and forget this.'

Logan sucked in smoke and removed the cigar from his lips. He glanced at the horseman. He knew he could never hide anything from Barker.

'Nope,' Logan admitted. 'We ain't quitting, Rem. We never quit when we can smell the sweet scent of money drifting on the air.'

'But the town sure has changed,' Barker said anxiously as he too tried to see if he could make sense of the new streets, which seemed to run off from the main street where the banks were. 'We ought to cut our losses and forget about them banks, Cole.'

'We got us enough gold coin to live like kings down in Mexico, Cole,' Curley pressed.

'For how long, though?' Logan asked through his cigar smoke. 'I reckon we might have us a few years living like royalty and then we're gonna have to ride back to get us more money.'

'So?'

'None of us is getting any younger, boys,' Logan

reasoned as he noted mentally that there was not one horse in the long street besides theirs. 'I don't hanker to being forced out of retirement when I'm too old to do the job properly. Nope. If we intend spending the last few years of our lives in luxury then we have to do this now.'

Barker shook his head. He could see the logic in Logan's words but had a bad feeling burning at his innards. 'I still reckon we might just be biting off a little too much here, Cole. This place ain't nothing like the towns we rob any more.'

Logan looked angry. 'We never quit, Rem. So they changed a few side streets. It don't matter none. All we do is ride back along this road to the livery and head for Mexico after we've robbed the banks.'

Barker leaned closer to Logan. 'We never ride back along wide streets after we've fleeced a bank, Cole. Never. It leaves our backs exposed to folks using them for target practice.'

Logan knew that his right-hand man was only repeating the things he himself had taught him. He sucked in more smoke and allowed it to linger for a while as his mind raced. If they worked this job as they normally did and rode into various alleyways after fleeing the main street they had to be certain they were not riding into dead-ends.

He eyed the people walking up and down the dusty boardwalks and grinned widely. 'We kill every man, woman and child that even looks like they know how to handle a hogleg, boys. Dead folks can't backshoot nobody. Right?'

His gang were still not convinced.

'Shaky? I want you to take five of the boys to the other end of Main Street,' Logan ordered. 'Check out every one of them sidestreets and alleys. Find out where they go and then ride back and tell us.'

Shaky Pete gave a nod. 'Where will you be, Cole?'

'The saloon yonder.' Logan jabbed his spurs and started his new horse moving again with his men flanking him. 'We'll be in the saloon opposite those juicy banks, Shaky. We'll be waiting for you boys to come back and tell us which of those streets lead out from Main Street back to the fork that leads into Mexico. We'll be buying us enough whiskey and provisions to fill them pack saddles. Savvy?'

Shaky Pete smiled. 'And drinking? Is we gonna do us some drinking before we start killing and robbing?'

'Damn right,' Logan roared. 'A whole lot of drinking.'

Logan led the rest of his riders slowly towards the saloon as Shaky and the others spurred hard and rode quickly to the other end of the long street. Logan pulled his reins hard to his left and steered the animal up to the hitching rail. He swiftly dismounted, looped his leathers around the weathered pole and waited as the remainder of his men copied his actions. One by one they stepped up under the overhang on to the boardwalk.

'I still don't like this, Cole.' Barker shook his head. 'We got us a fortune already. We don't really need no more loot.'

'I say we do, Rem,' Logan snarled. 'And I'm still the boss of this outfit. Right?'

The outlaws gave dutiful nods of their heads and trailed their leader through the swing doors into the saloon.

SEVENTEEN

Gene Adams stood like a granite statue watching the four men trail Johnny towards him through the dust. There was a fury inside him that he could not control. He raced forward, brushed the young cowboy aside and then slammed a clenched fist into the jaw of the first of the guards. The man went cartwheeling as the rancher turned towards the three others.

Before Adams was able to attack the trio of other terrified guards Rip and Larry leapt between them and held the furious rancher in check until he calmed down.

'You shot three of my boys,' Adams raged over the powerful shoulders of his wranglers. 'I should kill you. Whoever you are I should kill you.'

Johnny moved like a mountain lion toward the struggling rancher as his cohorts battled to restrain Adams. 'They're prison guards from Los Angelo, Gene. They happen to be chasing the same varmints as us but they got kinda confused and mistook us for them.'

'What? Prison guards?' Adams suddenly relaxed and tried to understand something which to him was beyond comprehension. 'We got ambushed by prison guards?'

'Yep.' Johnny lowered his head and stared at the ground before asking the fearful question which was burning inside him. 'Are any of our boys dead, Gene?'

There was a long pause. The rancher tried to control himself, but barely managed the feat.

Adams looked at the youngest of his cowboys. 'Not yet, Johnny, but Red's in a pretty bad way. We have to get them all to the nearest doc fast.'

'The closest sawbones is over in Fargo Springs,' Larry said firmly. 'Doc Bunston is his handle as I recall. Used to be another quack there called Richards but the poor critter got himself a real bad case of the shakes. He helps Bunston out, I'm told.'

'I sure hope he's used to cutting lead out of folks,' Rip said with a heavy sigh. 'Red must have three bullets in him.'

Johnny leaned against Rip and whispered. 'What about Happy and Tomahawk, Rip?'

'Just winged but they need sewing up,' the tall wrangler replied. 'They're bleeding like stuck pigs.'

The guard who had tasted the venom of the rancher's wrath held his jaw and managed to get up on to his feet. He shook his head as bloody spittle trailed from the corner of his mouth ran down his unshaven chin. 'My name's Spencer. Ted Spencer. These men are Pike, Walker and Dunn. I can't tell ya how sorry me and the boys are that we opened up on ya.'

Adams shook Larry and Rip off him and inhaled deeply. His eyes burned into Spencer for what felt like a lifetime to the guard. He then looked at Johnny. 'You go round up our horses, boy. The rest of us will help our wounded on to the horses of these guards.'

Spencer moved closer to his three fellow guards.

'That is OK with you, ain't it, Mr Spencer?' Adams snapped at the back of the groggy guard he had knocked off his feet.

Meekly, Spencer gestured his agreement.

The rancher placed gloved hands on the backs of Larry and Rip and steered them back to the canyon wall, where their three fellow Bar 10 cowboys were spread out on the sand. The ground had turned crimson as blood flowed from their several bullet holes. Adams swung on his heels, and raised an arm and pointed a finger at the four guards.

'Get them horses over here pronto,' the rancher shouted.

Spencer, Pike, Walker and Dunn obeyed the command. They knew that to argue would probably prove fatal. The guards manhandled their horses to the sand-coloured wall of rock as the rancher and his two uninjured cowboys carefully raised their pals off the sand and laid them over three of the high saddles. Adams had lifted Red off the sand single-handed and placed him face first across the shiny leather seat of the saddle. He grabbed the reins from Spencer's grip, rammed a boot into a stirrup and mounted the lathered up animal swiftly. He did not wait for the others. The seasoned rancher knew there was no time to waste. Red had to be taken to Doc Bunston fast.

Real fast.

With boot toes which barely reaching the stir-rups, Gene Adams balanced on the bedroll tied just behind the saddle cantle of Spencer's mount.

'You take Happy, Rip,' Adams said, then looked at Larry. 'And you bring Tomahawk.'

Both the Bar 10 wranglers touched the brims of their Stetsons.

The silver-haired rancher held the unconscious cowboy firmly in position with one hand whilst with the other he gripped tightly on to the reins.

Adams spurred. Then Rip and Larry spurred.

Ted Spencer grabbed the reins of the guards' remaining horse and mounted the animal just as he saw Johnny emerging through the hoof dust atop his pinto pony, leading the rest of the Bar 10's horseflesh.

'Where ya going, Ted?' Pike asked his fellow guard.

Spencer swung the head of the horse abruptly to his left and gritted his teeth. 'I'm going to try and help that big rancher, boys. I got me a feeling that if Cole Logan and his gang are in Fargo Springs, he's gonna need all the help he can get.'

The prison guard whipped the horse's tail with his long leathers. The animal responded and began trailing the three others through the heat haze towards the distant settlement.

Johnny Puma reined in as he reached the trio of guards and glared down at them.

'C'mon. Get ya sorry backsides up on these nags, boys,' he ordered. 'We got us a real big fight brewing by my figuring. Maybe this time ya might shoot the right varmints.'

The guards scrambled up on to the unfamiliar, high-shouldered Bar 10 horses. Johnny rammed his spurs into the pinto.

Within a heartbeat they were all riding through the dust in pursuit of the others.

There was indeed a war brewing and each of them knew that it was waiting only a few miles ahead of them in Fargo Springs. As their horses thundered along the sunbaked trail Johnny Puma realized there would be no heroes at the end of the coming battle, but there would be dead.

An awful lot of dead.

EIGHTEEN

The main street suddenly erupted into venomous fury. Fargo Springs had never seen or heard anything to equal it. Bullets tore from the barrels of the mounted outlaws' guns as the three merciless horsemen began to clear the streets of any and all people who happened to be within range of their .45s. Men, women and even children were targeted by the six riders as their fellow bank robbers went about their work and stormed both banks simultaneously. The screams of the dead and dying echoed along the thoroughfare whilst Shaky Pete kept the riders firing at every living soul who got too close.

Two muffled explosions from inside the banks sent clouds of billowing smoke out into the bright afternoon sunlight. The entire street shook as the tremors of short-fused dynamite sticks sent shock waves through the stunned settlement.

Sheriff Dan Carver ran from his office clutching a double-barrelled scattergun in both hands. For twelve years the lawman had served Fargo Springs without ever having had to do anything more dangerous than break up a fistfight on a Saturday night. Now the forty year old sheriff was running out into a crowd of people who were all fleeing the centre of town. Dan Carver paused for the briefest of moments, screwing up his eyes as people ran away from the mayhem.

'What's happening?' Carver shouted at the terrified souls, but none of them dared stop to answer.

The sheriff spat at the ground and set on towards the smoke that was rising up into the street beyond the running townsfolk. He realized that when there was trouble and people were running it meant that a lawman headed in the opposite direction. He headed towards the shooting. He was paid to do what no one else in Fargo Springs either would or could do.

Carver had barely walked fifty yards when he saw them.

The six horsemen were firing their weaponry at anything that moved. Even at the backs of unarmed people who were fleeing their wrath. The closer Carver got to where the outlaws were shooting the more bodies he saw. Even the curling smoke that lingered over the main street could not hide the dead and wounded from the lawman's startled eyes.

The sheriff cocked both hammers of his hefty scattergun and hoisted its barrel until it was aimed in the rough direction of the carnage.

'Drop them guns,' Carver yelled out.

Shaky Pete swung his mount around and stared over the scattering of wounded souls along the street at the man with the shining star pinned to his chest. A sly grin was etched on his hardened features as he signalled to the two outlaws on either side of him.

'Davy! Bill!' Shaky called out, then pointed his smoking gun barrel at the lawman. 'He's all yours. I gotta reload.'

The pair of riders whipped their mounts and galloped down the long street towards the terrified sheriff. They raised their six-shooters and both fired at the same moment. Even with their horses in full flight their accuracy was still keen.

Dan Carver felt both of the bullets which tore into his chest and turned him on his heels until he dropped on to one knee. The lawman swallowed hard but there was no spittle in his dry mouth, only blood. He coughed and more blood splattered from his mouth over the big scattergun in his hands.

Thinking the sheriff was helpless the pair of outlaws rode closer to their kneeling target. Carver heard their hammers being cocked for action and mustered every scrap of his dwindling strength. He raised the twin-barrelled scattergun. He did not aim. There was no time to aim.

No time to think.

There was only enough time to fire.

Carver dragged back on the huge weapon's triggers.

Two powerful blasts of buckshot-filled flames erupted from the long barrels of the big gun. It sounded like thunder. The kick from the recoil was as hard as any mule could have delivered. Sheriff Carver felt the smoking scattergun slide from his blood-soaked hands. The gunsmoke rose into the hot air and allowed the dying lawman to see what he had just done in all its colourful detail. With half-closed eyes Carver stared at the result of his lethal handiwork.

The deadly buckshot had torn the two riders to shreds and what was left of them was spread out across the sand only ten feet from where Carver himself lay. Their horses had not been any luckier than the riders. They were on their sides kicking at the air as life slipped from them as quickly as did their gore. The lawman felt no satisfaction in what he had just done. He stared down at his chest at the sheriff's six-pointed star. It was quickly being submerged in a lake of the lawman's blood.

Totally stunned by the sudden loss of two of the gang, Shaky Pete snapped his smoking gun chamber back into the body of his Colt. He dragged back on his hammer. As soon as the hammer had fully locked into position Shaky raised his weapon and held it at arm's length. He aimed and fired at the man with the star pinned to his vest.

A spray of scarlet blood cascaded from Carver's skull and sparkled in the bright sunshine. It fell like rain over what was left of the lawman and the other bodies that surrounded him.

Dan Carver was knocked backwards by the power of the deadly bullet. He fell on to the ground. His arms were outstretched yet limp like those of a child's rag doll.

Carver lay motionless.

He was dead.

Reaching the edge of Fargo Springs Gene Adams dragged rein only a moment or two before Rip and Larry outside Doc Bunston's small house, which stood within spitting distance of the big livery stable. A cloud of choking hoof dust billowed over the weathered structure as the silver-haired rancher dismounted and carefully eased his severely wounded cowpuncher off the saddle. Adams took the weight of the still unconscious wrangler, turned and approached the doctor's door. With Red Evans cradled in his arms Adams was about to kick at the door when it unexpectedly opened. Adams nodded at the tall, dark-haired Doc Bunston as the medical man steered the rancher towards a long flat table in the middle of the parlour.

'What's happening today?' Bunston asked, glancing keenly at the cowboy in the rancher's strong arms.

'Gunplay, Doc,' Adams replied as he lay Red down.

'I'll take good care of him, Mr Adams,' Bunston said confidently.

'You know me?' the rancher sounded surprised.

'Everyone knows the boss of the Bar 10,' the doctor replied. He pushed Adams aside and tore the wounded cowboy's shirt apart, revealing the blood-covered torso and the bullet holes. 'This is bad.'

'I figured that.' Adams turned just as Rip and Larry helped Tomahawk and Happy into the gloomy interior of the house and sat them down on hard chairs.

Doc Bunston glanced at both seated cowboys. 'Don't worry about them. They're just winged, Mr Adams. This young cowboy, however, needs urgent surgery.'

The rancher ran a sleeve across his face. He could not hide his concern. Then the doctor yelled out at the back room of the house.

'Doctor Richards. Can you get in here? I need your help.'

A weatherworn figure emerged from the rear of the small building. He was holding a bowl filled with hot water. 'I heard you, damn it. Seems like a man can't ever retire in these parts. Somebody is always getting themselves shot. Get my instruments out of my bag. Reckon we got us some digging to do.'

'Digging?' The younger doctor repeated the word.

'For bullets, boy,' Doc Richards nodded, pulled a bottle of whiskey from his pants pockets and placed it beside the cowboy's head. 'For bullets.'

Then the sound of distant gunfire filled the ranchers' ears once more. Adams looked at his men, who were covered in blood. Their own as well as that of their saddle pals.

Adams touched the brim of his black hat. 'Doc Richards? Is that you?'

'Of course it is, Adams.' Richards gestured rudely with his hands. 'Go away.'

'You heard him. Get out.' Bunston yelled at the cowboys. 'Let us work.'

'Rip, Larry,' Adams said from the corner of his mouth before making for the door and the bright sunshine beyond. 'C'mon.'

Just as Gene Adams and the Bar 10 cowboys emerged from the dark interior of the doctors' house, Johnny and the guards rode up behind the guards' horses. Johnny swiftly dismounted. He cast an eye in the direction of the livery stable opposite and the trail-weary horses inside it.

'What ya looking at?' Ted Spencer asked the cowboy as he too dropped to the ground and moved close to the curious cowboy.

'Them horses that blacksmith is tending are in worse condition than yours, Spencer,' Johnny observed. He walked towards the wide open doorway. He rested beside one of the doors and stared at the horses. There were twelve of them and they had been ridden hard and mercilessly by men would did not value them. The youngster glanced at the prison guard. 'They've gotta be the outlaws' horses.'

'Ya right,' Spencer agreed.

With the distant shooting still ringing out closer to the centre of Fargo Springs Adams called out to the youngster. 'Get here, Johnny. You as well, Mr Spencer.'

The cowboy and Spencer ran back to the grey-faced rancher as Adams grabbed his saddle horn and mounted his chestnut mare. He looked down at Johnny, who was pointing at the livery stable.

'Spit it out, boy,' Adams drawled.

'Them outlaws' horses are over in that livery, Gene.'

The rancher sighed and waved a fist angrily at the seven men who encircled him.

'Listen. Are you all deaf?' Adams raged. 'Can't you hear that gunplay?'

For the first time since they had reached the outskirts of town the men became aware of the constant gunfire which was echoing all around them.

'Holy cow. That is shooting. A lot of shooting,' Johnny gasped and briefly looked heavenward. 'Damn. I figured there was a storm brewing, Gene. I just thought it was thunder.'

'There is a storm brewing, Johnny,' Adams nodded as he listened to the sound of more and more shots ringing out in the distance. 'A storm like none of us has ever tangled with before.'

'The Logan gang must have gotten themselves fresh mounts. I reckon they're now robbing the bank,' Spencer said. He climbed back on top of one of their horses. 'Is that how you see it, Mr Adams?'

'Yep,' Adams growled furiously. With his gloved hands he gathered up his reins. 'And they'll be taking whatever they can steal from that bank, as well as the Circle J gold coin down into Mexico so they can live like a herd of damn kings for the rest

143

of their days. That is if somebody don't stop them first.'

Pike looked wary. 'This ain't our fight.'

'It is our fight, Pike,' Spencer disagreed. 'We owe them dead boys back at Los Angelo that much. We come looking for Logan and the bastards who bust him free from jail, didn't we?'

Pike shrugged, then nodded. 'Yeah. Ya right.'

Rip and Larry mounted their horses and swung the animals around until they were facing the centre of town. Adams looked at the riders who surrounded him and gave a nod.

'C'mon, boys,' the rancher snorted. 'I figure it's time we spoiled Cole Logan's plans once and for all.'

The eight horsemen spurred and thundered away from the small house and the livery stable. They were heading to where the sound of gunfire was loudest. With every stride of their horses the noise of the ferocious gunfire grew ever greater.

The Logan gang did not know it yet but not everyone inside the unmarked boundaries of Fargo Springs was as defenceless as those they had already slain. Unlike most of those who had fled in the opposite direction to the outlaws' hot lead, the

144

eight determined horsemen were actually heading directly towards the horrific sound of the outlaws' ruthless shooting.

There was but one thought in all their minds.

Retribution.

NINETEEN

The dead and wounded were mounting up as the outlaws ran from each bank at nearly the same time. Cole Logan led the way to their horses as Curley Jones and the others filled the pack saddles with sacks of gold coin. Rem Barker trailed his cohorts from the smaller of the banks, his guns still blazing at those who had survived the gang's initial attack. As was their way, the Logan gang seldom left any witnesses alive in or close to the banks once they had robbed them.

With half a dozen guns hanging from leather laces suspended around his wide neck Barker kept firing one weapon after another at any man, woman or child who got close enough to recognize him. Since he had started riding with the notorious Logan gang he alone had never been identified as one of the most lethal bank robbers alive. Barker lived by the simple rule that if you killed anyone who got a good look at you, then there would never be any witnesses who could send you to the gallows. Barker kept firing his arsenal as his fellow gang members brought bags of gold coin from the smouldering remnants of the banks and secured them to their packhorses. There was far more gold than any of the outlaws had ever imagined. Enough for a hundred lifetimes.

The air was thick with acrid gunsmoke as each of the ten surviving bank robbers expertly went about their duties. Each of the gang knew his job and, until the moment two of their number had been felled by Sheriff Carver's scattergun, they had never lost a single man.

The dry afternoon air was filled with smoke as Logan mounted his new horse. He watched as the last of his gang followed suit. The steel-coloured eyes of the outlaw leader were said to be as keen as that of an eagle. They never missed anything within their range. Logan sat silently atop his horse reloading his smoking weapons as his gang filled their packhorse's saddles with bag after bag of golden eagles.

Then Logan spied his two dead followers just beyond Shaky Pete. He was stunned.

Logan spurred and rode towards Shaky Pete as the mounted outlaw surveyed the long street for another target to shoot at. Logan could not hide his anger or horror that two of their number were lying dead beside their stricken horses. He dragged back on his reins and stopped his mount.

'What happened?' Logan yelled at Shaky Pete, aiming his gun barrel at the two dead outlaws.

'Damn sheriff cut loose with a scattergun, Cole,' Shaky said in a low hissing snarl. 'There weren't nothing I could do. I killed him, though. Killed him real good.'

Cole Logan rose in his saddle and stared at the dead lawman. The bullet hole in his temple was still leaking gore like a primed pump.

'Ya should have killed him before he opened up with that scattergun, Shaky,' Logan ranted. 'I don't like losing men at the best of times but to lose them to a star-packer with a damn scattergun riles me.'

Barker threw himself up on to his saddle and swung the skittish mount around as his cold eyes searched for anything left alive that he could shoot. 'Reckon we got what we come for, Cole. I'm for high-tailing it.'

The words had barely left the lips of Logan's right-hand man than suddenly the sound of pounding hoofs filled the long street. The bank robbers swung their horses to face the steady sound of the approaching horsemen but it was not as easy as it seemed. The noise of the hoofs appeared to be coming from all around the outlaws.

That was because they were. Adams had spread his riders out. Only he and Spencer came thundering into the main street from the direction that the Logan gang had used to reach the banks. The rest of the intrepid Bar 10 cowboys and prison guards had spread out and were descending on the town's main artery from four different directions at once. Unlike the outlaws they had not been confused by the rebuilding work that had altered Fargo Springs.

Infuriated, Logan stood in his stirrups and stared at each of the approaching riders in turn. His eyes darted from one alleyway to another as horsemen converged on Main Street with their guns blazing.

'What'll we do, Cole?' Curley yelled out as he fought with the heavily laden packhorse tied to his own unfamiliar mount's saddle. Neither animal would budge.

'Kill them!' Logan screamed out at the top of his lungs.

The outlaws did not require telling twice. They knew how to kill almost as well as they knew how to rob banks. They started firing at the horsemen who were coming at them from all sides.

Bullets spewed their venom in all directions from every one of the riders' gun barrels. A swarm of crazed hornets could not have created more confusion. Tapers of lethal lightning rods cut across the town's main street in search of moving targets. The targets themselves refused to remain still long enough for anyone to aim their weapons, and kept firing. The good and the bad were fanning their gun hammers relentlessly with equal ferocity. Outlaws buckled and fell from their saddles.

At the very moment when a guard fell into the dust Rip felt his high-shouldered horse buckle beneath him. The cowboy went hurtling over its neck as the animal crashed into the ground. The wrangler rolled away from the dying horse, then lay on his belly as bullets kicked up the ground all about him. Even shaken up and badly bruised, Rip continued to fire his six-shooters at the outlaws.

The outlaw Curley once again spurred his mount but the packhorse he had tethered to his saddle fender refused to budge. The outlaw swung around and was then lifted up into the air by a volley of bullets which came from three different directions. The dead outlaw fell to the ground as Barker rode up to the gold-laden packhorse. The outlaw kept firing one of his guns at the same time as he tried vainly to free its reins from Curley's saddle. A bullet caught Barker in his shoulder. He watched in horror as his fingers spread and the gun fell into the bloodstained sand.

'I'm hit,' Barker yelled out.

Gene Adams spurred hard, drove his tall mare through the acrid gunsmoke and then leapt from his saddle. He caught the wounded Barker around the shoulders. Both men crashed into the ground.

Although winded, Rem Barker managed to find another of his guns with his good hand. He turned and fired in one swift action.

A bullet burned a hole through Adams's coat. The rancher smashed a clenched fist into the outlaw's jaw, then forced himself back up on to his feet. He saw Barker's thumb claw back on the .45s hammer again, and he drew one of his own guns. Two shots rang out. Only one had found its target. Barker fell on his back, staring at the sky with dead eyes.

The rancher stepped over Barker's body and saw Cole Logan as the outlaw leader raised a gun and aimed at the approaching Johnny.

Adams had no time to think. There was only time to act.

The rancher fanned his gun hammer twice. Two red-hot plumes of fiery lead were sent across the main street toward the lethal horseman. Both bullets caught Logan in his chest. Adams watched as Logan was knocked over his cantle and slid lifelessly over the tail of his mount. The leader of the infamous Logan gang fell face first into the churned-up sand.

Johnny steered his pinto through the mayhem with the skill that only cowboys ever achieve. He reached the rancher and stopped his pony.

'Get up behind me, Gene.'

Suddenly, before Adams could respond there was a massive explosion halfway along the street. What was left of Shaky Pete went flying high into the air as the last of his dynamite sticks exploded in his saddle-bags. The prison guard, Spencer, stared at his smoking gun and then at the result of his wayward shot.

'Reckon I did that,' Spencer said as the last pair of outlaws drove through the gunsmoke with their guns blasting in all directions.

Protecting the rancher, Johnny held his pony in check beside Adams and drew one of his Colts. He fanned its hammer until its chamber was empty. Each of his shots had been deadly accurate and had hit each of the riders in turn. They had fallen like leaves from a dead tree. The battle had lasted less than two minutes.

The gunsmoke slowly lifted to reveal the dead. Every one of the Logan gang lay amid the bodies of the innocent townsfolk they had slaughtered. Adams moved forward and grabbed the reins of his mare.

'Reckon we won, Gene,' Johnny said.

'I don't feel like we won, boy.' Adams stared at the horror which surrounded them. Only one of the guards had not survived. Larry and Rip walked slowly through the bodies towards the rancher as Spencer, Pike and Walker steered their horses towards the grim-faced Adams as he stepped into his stirrup and eased himself back on to his saddle. 'I'm heading back to find out how our boys are.'

The three guards watched as the four cowboys rode away.

They did not feel victorious either.

FINALE

The sun was at last beginning to set. The sky above Fargo Springs seemed to be aflame as ripples of crimson spread over the remote settlement. Gene Adams and his three battle-weary cowboys sat on the sand outside the doctors' small house and waited for the two medical men to finish their work. It had been two hours since the rancher and his men had confronted the Logan gang, but to each of them it seemed that far less time had elapsed.

The door opened and Happy and Tomahawk staggered out into the reddish light. Both cowboys had been patched up. Happy had an arm in a sling and Tomahawk's head was swathed in bandages, hiding the graze which had knocked him senseless.

Both reached their pals and eased themselves down on to the still hot sand next to them.

Adams sighed and was about to speak when both the doctors trailed the wranglers out into the last rays of the day's sunlight. Bunston rested his back against the wooden wall of the house as Richards exhaled loudly. Both were soaked in sweat.

The rancher rose to his feet and moved between the two doctors. He looked at the older man.

'How's Red, Doc?' Adams asked nervously.

Doc Richards' eyes looked at the tall man who stood beside him clutching his black Stetson in his gloved hands. He smiled.

'He'll be fine,' Richards confirmed. 'I managed to get all the bullets out of him and stop the bleeding, Gene.'

Bunston eased himself away from the wall and walked to the rancher. 'He means that we cut the bullets out, Mr Adams.'

Richards pushed Adams out of the way and stood eyeballing his fellow medic. 'You only cut one of them bullets out. I found two of the damn things.'

'I'd have found them,' Bunston protested.

Doc Richards rocked with laughter. 'Eventually you might have found them. Hell! Without me you'd not have found the damn patient.'

Fuming, Doc Bunston marched back into the house with the older man on his heels. 'You ain't even managed to find your way out of town yet, Richards. You don't even know what the word retire means. You're like a ghost. You like nothing better than haunting folks.'

Gene Adams was smiling as he stood over the seated cowboys. 'At least Red's OK. I was kinda worried. I reckon they both saved Red's life.'

A dazed Tomahawk looked up at the rancher from the bandages which half-hid his eyes. 'Has ya hired us a cook yet, Gene boy?'

Adams shook his head. 'Nope. I'd plumb forgotten about that, you old goat.'

A still confused Tomahawk looked at the others seated beside him. 'Ya ain't? Then what the hell have ya bin doing since we got here, ya young whippersnapper?'

Adams lifted Tomahawk up off the sand. He stared into the wrinkled features and beamed. 'You want to find a saloon, old-timer?'

'Darn tooting I do.' Tomahawk winked. 'I already got me a hangover so I might as well do some whiskey sipping.'

'You never know, we might find us a cook in one of the saloons in town,' Gene Adams mused as he led his cowboys away from the doctors' small house. He rested a hand on Tomahawk's bony shoulder. 'I might even find out how Cookie bust his leg.'